THE RED-TAILED SPIRIT

THE RED-TAILED SPIRIT

Bob McCurdy

Prairie Viking Press
Westby, Wisconsin

Published by
Prairie Viking Press

ISBN 978-0-9888794-6-1
ISBN 0-9888794-6-8

Printed in the U.S.A.

The Red-tailed Spirit is Published by:
Prairie Viking Press
www.sherpe.com

Cover Photo by Bob McCurdy

Also by Bob McCurdy:
Starting Over
The Dog Who Took His Man For A Walk
Sometimes You Get The Bear
The Grandpa Who Wasn't
An August To Remember
The Butternut Hawk
If You Don't Ask

ACKNOWLEDGEMENTS

My thanks to Kyran Clark for his painstaking proof reading. He's also a master at challenging discrepancies and or inconsistencies. He's good at being able to step back and see the forest.

Howard Sherpe and I are close in age, but he's still working a full-time day job. Despite that, he manages to make time to meticulously go through my books getting them print-ready.

In a previous life, Howard had his own business designing advertising in Madison. Seven years ago he was offered employment in his hometown and moved back to Westby where he lives on a corner of the farm he grew up on.

Because of his contacts in the Madison area, he was able to engage an outstanding printing firm, The Printing Place in Middleton, Wisconsin, to produce the finished product. This is the eighth novel they've done for me. Thanks, guys. Well done.

Chapter 1

Somewhere in the central highlands of Vietnam, December 24, 1967. It was monsoon season, the rain was so torrential the two low-flying, in-coming rescue helicopters could hardly be heard, let alone seen until they were almost over head. Their mission was to extract six Army rangers who were members of an elite team known as LRRPs (Long Range Reconnaissance Patrol). The team's goal was to find enemy positions, its size and movement, then disappear and return with the information they'd gathered. The last thing they wanted was to let their presence be known. They traveled light. Their only weapons were their M-16 rifles, ten clips of ammunition, two grenades apiece and K-bar knives. They had three days of K-rations and water purification tablets. They'd been on a number of previous missions together infiltrating the jungles deep into enemy territory. They were far from their base of operations in the central highlands, a mountainous region in South Vietnam close to the Laotian border. Now they were under fire. They'd discovered a large unit of Vietcong that were hunkered down waiting for the rain to subside.

They'd completed their reconnaissance and were in the process of withdrawing when one of the rangers triggered an enemy grenade that had been rigged with a thin tripwire. The grenade had been set a couple of feet off the ground to inflict maximum injury. He knew immediately what he'd done. He dove forward hoping to minimize his injuries, not wanting to become a serious liability to his comrades, or to die. The grenade exploded a moment later. The shrapnel tore off the right heel of his boot and severed his Achilles tendon. Most of the rest of the fragments grazed or penetrated the back of his legs and buttocks at sharp angles. Two of his comrades grabbed him and began dragging him toward the edge of the dense jungle forest. There was a broad grassy opening adjacent to the forest. The other three took defensive positions. The men had their weapons on semi-auto. They were all expert marksmen. They knew to pick their targets, not to waste precious ammunition by firing indiscriminately. Lieutenant Willis Morrissey carried a small radio-sending device that could be activated if the patrol unit required emergency 'extraction'. This was the first time he'd had to use it. They'd always been able to make their way back on their own.

He triggered the Emergency Position Indicating Radio Beacon sender EPIRB, hoping there was military aircraft in the vicinity able to pick up the signal. It was the only chance they had of being rescued. It's signal served both as MAYDAY and as a homing device able to guide the rescue choppers to their exact location.

The men knew, even if the signal was received, it would be at least an hour before help arrived. With these weather conditions they might be SOL. They also knew it wouldn't be possible for them to sustain an engagement with a VC force of this size for any length of time. To make things worse, they knew even if help did arrive, the rescue choppers had no way of knowing what the situation was, the choppers themselves were going to be in jeopardy. Lieutenant Morrissey, 'LT' as he was called, was 'going by the book'. It was his job to make every effort to try to get them out alive. He felt ambivalent, knowing his decision might end up costing several additional lives.

Figarro and Dennison worked to administer first aid to their wounded comrade, Sgt. Grant. He lay face down with his wounded leg elevated to help stanch the bleeding, as the rain pelted down. The visibility was probably less than a hundred yards. If the choppers showed up, the rescue would need to be executed as quickly as possible. Every second meant increased risk. Grant apologized for getting them into this mess. The sound of the rain dampened any other sounds. The temperature was in the low eighties, but they were on the brink of shivering because of the cold drenching rain.

They held their positions sharing the same hope. Maybe the grenade blast hadn't been heard, and they hadn't been detected. Even taking into account the dampening effect of the rain and the dense foliage of the jungle, that scenario was unlikely. Time passed with excruciating slowness.

The intensity of the down-pour had one advantage, it was serving to make them a little less easy to track. However, because Grant had been dragged, the disturbed and broken foliage would be a dead giveaway to a skilled tracker. This was Charlie's turf. The VC knew the jungles. They were not a group of urban boy scouts on a weekend in the woods. The team had to assume contact was inevitable. They knew the cards were stacked against them. Charlie had all of the advantages, including time. None of these men could be regarded as foolhardy, or stupid. Yet, none of them would have been able to offer a reasonable explanation for why they risked themselves to go on these missions.

The rain began to diminish in intensity, not uncommon even during the peak of monsoon season. The rain might stop entirely for two or three hours, sometimes even most of a day, only to resume by unleashing another relentless deluge. Without the waterfall-like roar of the rain pouring down on the broad waxy leaves of the jungle foliage, nuances of forest sound became discernible. The men were tired, wet, and hungry, but they were also 'wired' and alert to the slightest movement that seemed out of the ordinary. The rule in a situation like this was no sudden or obvious movement that would give your position away. That meant they didn't even slap a mosquito.

An hour passed, still nothing. Each man could see the man to either side of him. If anyone of them detected anything unusual he would signal the others with subtle hand gestures. A light mist began to fall again. From the corner of his eye LT picked up a signal from Green, a lean, quiet black man on his third tour. LT focused his attention on Green who had his hand raised just enough to be visible. LT gave Green a nod of acknowledgment. He signaled McLeod to his right and Figarro to his left, he cocked his wrist pointing in the direction of the movement. McLeod and Figarro in turn alerted the others in similar fashion. Each man eased the safeties off their weapons and slowly positioned themselves.

The drizzle began to increase into a steady rain serving to mute the more subtle forest sounds. Suddenly three figures appeared like apparitions emerging from some steamy under world. They moved cautiously, slowly scanning the foliage, obviously tracking the path left by Grant's removal. They wore wide-brimmed, round woven grass hats that stood out in contrast to the dark green of the jungle. The three VC carried their AK-47s at the ready. One of them stopped and signaled the others. He appeared to be sniffing the air. Because a lot of GIs smoked, or used scented deodorants or insect repellents, they could often be detected in the moist, still air of the jungles by smell. Will thought, *Charlie has to be wondering who we are. They have to know we're a small unit, we're a long way from home, and they're wondering why we're here. They can't risk letting any of us escape. They'll do whatever it takes to kill all of us.*

The rangers knew these three trackers were point

men, sent to locate their position. Others would be close behind. They held their fire hoping the point men would pass them by. It would buy them a little more time. It wouldn't take long before the scouts figured out no one had gone out into the tall grass beyond the forest. That would light the fuse. The larger force would swoop in as soon as contact was made. The best they could hope for was to inflict as much damage as possible before they ran out of ammunition and were overtaken. Charlie wasn't going to retreat even if they suffered a number of casualties. Morrissey, Figarro, and Green each had a target in their sights. These were three dead Vietcong.

A few moments later six more figures became visible. The rain seemed to be increasing. At a nod from LT, each man took a breath, held it and squeezed their triggers. It was an almost simultaneous crack. A volley of seven or eight more shots were fired. All nine of the targets fell. The jungle became silent except for the sound of the rain. Their position was obvious now. The loss of nine of their comrades would add vengeance to the equation.

It was at that moment the two helicopters swooped by low overhead. One of them dropped down about thirty yards from the edge of the jungle barely touching the chest deep grass. The other chopper hovered broadside to the forest about twenty feet above the ground. A machine gunner stood in the open door ready to open fire. The chopper pilots kept their engine rpms up to enable a rapid lift off. LT gave the signal, Figarro and Dennison moved quickly dragging Grant into the tall grass. McLeod and LT maintained positions at the very edge of the forest to provide cover. Suddenly a bunch of VC popped up several yards from them and began firing. The three remaining Rangers returned fire, dropping half a dozen of them. LT yelled, "Go, Go, Go," The two men immediately left the forest and began wading through the tall wet grass as if they were in slow motion. LT jammed a fresh clip into his rifle and shot two more advancing VC. He turned and began running himself. When he was about ten yards from the forest edge the machine gunner in the nearest chopper opened fire directing a rain of 50 caliber bullets at the edge of the forest.

Will heard return fire coming from the jungle. Two or three bullets whizzed by him as he waded through the tall grass. One of them grazed his helmet knocking it off into the grass. The impact felt like a hard slap on the side of his head, knocking him sideways and causing him to fall. He got back to his feet slightly dazed. Driven by a rush of adrenalin, he plowed his way forward, panting hard. He was almost there. The helicopter pilot increased the trim of the rotor blades and gave the engine increased throttle just as Will reached the chopper entrance. The rain was pouring down. With a sudden lurch the chopper started to move upward. Will was only part way in and before anyone could grab him he slid backward. He caught the landing rail with one hand. Letting go of his rifle he strained to get hold of it with both hands. The chopper was about thirty feet off the ground when a bullet slammed into the right side of his flack jacket knocking the wind out of him, and causing him to lose his grip. His fall was off-balance and he landed straight legged to his right side. He heard the snap of a bone in his lower leg, accompanied by a sickening jolt of excruciating pain. He instantly knew his leg was broken. He looked down to see the bone had torn through his pant leg and was protruding. He tried to reach for one of the grenades attached to his vest and experienced a shock of dreadful pain in his right shoulder. He gasped, lying in a drenched heap, trying to understand what this other pain was. The chopper he'd tried to board disappeared into the heavy down pour.

He heard machine gun fire and the engine throb from the other chopper just before he lost consciousness.

Chapter 2

When Will gained consciousness he was completely disoriented. He had no idea where he was or how long he'd been out. It was raining, he was soaked and shivering and in terrible pain. He realized he was in a sitting position. He tried to open his eyes. It was like they'd been glued shut. Even his lips were stuck together. His upper body was wracked with pain. He felt nothing from his thighs on down. He tipped his head back hoping the rain would dissolve whatever it was that kept him from being able to part his lips and open his eyes. He needed water. His hands were tied in front of him, but something was in the way. He couldn't use them to touch his face. He was finally able to open his lips and take in some water. He managed to open one of his eyes. When he was finally able to focus he realized he was in a small bamboo cage. His legs hung out of it. He deduced the cage was hanging, which accounted for the lack of feeling in his legs. Their numbness was the result of sitting in one position for a prolonged period of time. He had no way of knowing the numbness was a blessing. He tried to make sense of his situation. He finally figured out that the cage he was in was hanging from a tree. He saw a similar cage hanging from another tree several feet away. He gradually came to the realization he'd been taken prisoner. Was he alone? Were there others? Where were his captors?

He tried to remember what had happened. An image came to him of struggling to reach a chopper. He wasn't sure, but he thought he'd made it. Then it vanished. Maybe there wasn't any chopper. Maybe he'd imagined help had arrived. Had they been overtaken? Where was he? Where are the others? Are they dead? How did he get here? He felt dazed and numb, in a stupefied state. He felt a sense of infantile helplessness and he wanted to cry out, but to whom? He became aware of a terrible stench and was finally able to focus his mind enough to realize it was the smell of urine and feces and body odor. It took him a while to come to the further realization the smell was emanating from the cage he was in. It came from himself. He was sitting in his own waste. He'd soiled himself, how many times? *"How long have I been here? Where am I?"* As his mind slowly began to process, he tried to assess his situation. The cage he was in was perhaps three feet off the ground. He tried to raise his right hand, but he felt such agonizing pain he almost lost consciousness again. He was able to move his left arm somewhat, but even that movement triggered pain on his right side. He leaned forward and was finally able to work his left hand to his face. He discovered he had a tangled growth of beard. He'd not shaved for the three or four days during the time the patrol had been out. This was way beyond the stubble of a five o'clock shadow. He concluded whatever happened took place a couple of weeks ago, maybe longer. Will sucked the moisture that had collected on his mustache. He cupped his left hand to his lower lip and collected sips of rain. Even swallowing was painful. He did this for a long time wondering if this might be the first water he'd received since... since when? Since what?

The rain continued, and he was gradually able to extend his ability to focus beyond himself and the cage. He appeared to be in some sort of encampment. He was alone. There was no sign of life. There weren't even any articles of clothing or equipment. It was apparent he'd been abandoned by his captors. How long ago had they left? He was slowly able to gather some recollection of trying to get to a helicopter. He remembered reaching it just as it began to ascend, and his falling. *What happened after that? I must have been captured. Am I alone? Where are the others?* Eventually he spotted two lean-tos that had been fashioned from bamboo and had foliage stacked on top to provide shelter from the incessant rain. It looked like some layers of grass had been laid down as bedding under structures. He tried to move, protecting his right arm as much as possible. He tried leaning himself to the left, his back had been against the rear of the cage. He guessed the cage was eighteen or twenty inches square and perhaps four feet high.

When he shifted himself it caused the structure of the cage to shift as well. He saw the side he was facing pop loose at the top. He studied this with the dullness of a battered prize fighter. Somehow, he reached a vague conclusion. He leaned himself forward enough to press his head against the front of the cage. It seemed to give way a bit. He painfully moved his head back, and then tried butting the front again with his head. The whole side gave way on his third try and it fell out. Will's legs were positioned between the bamboo rungs. As it fell one of them caught on the protruding bone of his right leg. He screamed as a bolt of intense searing pain blasted through him like he'd been struck by lightning. He was on the brink of losing consciousness again, and probably for good. In desperation he threw his upper body forward. The momentum carried him out of the cage. He toppled onto the side of the cage and the grass lashings broke loose. He lay amid a pile of bamboo sticks and mud. Later he would reflect on the good fortune of its fragile construction, noting that, otherwise, it could have snapped the protruding bone off entirely. He lay gasping in the wreckage. By the time he was able to gather himself to the task of what to do next, it was almost dark. He'd wondered before if it was early morning, or closer to evening. Darkness came swiftly in the tropics, and even swifter in the jungles. He began trying to drag himself toward one of the lean-tos. It was well after dark before he was finally able to get himself part way under the closest one.

Several times during the course of his torturous journey he'd stopped to drink from puddles. He lay with just his upper body out of the rain. One of the thoughts that crossed his mind was why he wasn't experiencing any pangs of hunger. He wondered if he'd received any food from his captors. *Where are they? What if they return and find me here?* He wondered if they'd be returning, or had they just left him to die. He envisioned a scenario where his captors had just said, 'fuck him, he's not worth wasting a bullet on. We'll just leave the Yankee bastard here to die and be devoured by some predator'.

When he awakened again it was beginning to grow light. It was misting lightly. He felt cold. He was lying face down unable to even roll himself over. A thought began to unfold. He needed to find a way to end his life. *Even if Charlie doesn't return, what are my chances of surviving like this? I'm so messed up I can't possibly get myself out of here. I'll end up starving to death, or some raging goddamn infection is going to kill me.* He came upon the idea of trying to create a large enough puddle in the mud he could drown himself. *Let the damn rain be my weapon*. He fell asleep and while he slept the rain stopped. When he awakened again he felt warm. He opened his eyes to a brightness he couldn't identify. It finally occurred to him the sun was shining. It wasn't raining. There was a layer of steam rising across the open area of the encampment. For a while he savored the warmth, only to then realize his plan of drowning himself was being delayed. *'The Goddamn Gods are fucking with me'*. He lay there unable to move. He felt hungry, but it was a cautious hunger, the kind that one feels after having vomited so often you're not sure about being able to hold anything down.

After a while he forced himself to move into a different position. He couldn't get himself upright. He painfully rolled to the left until he was able to get on his back. It took him almost another half hour of painful deliberate, maneuvering to get himself to one of the vertical up-rights of the lean-to and into a sitting position. In the process he'd peed himself twice. He sat there panting with his head cocked back as if he were sunbathing, or perhaps begging for relief. He thought of Leslie, his wife. He pictured her only briefly before the dreadful pain brought him back to the awful reality of his condition. He hoped no one would ever discover his remains to know how he'd died.

He became aware the grasses lining the floor of the lean-to had seeds attached. Using his left hand he stripped a few of the seeds, brought them to his mouth, and began chewing them. He repeated this process several times. *They must have some nutritional value, however minute.* He almost smiled to himself. *Not exactly what a condemned man would request for his last meal.* He found himself amused. It was ironic that he was concerning himself with taking in any kind of sustenance given his doomed situation, and his desire to try to end his life.

Will lay in a stupor until finally retreating into sleep. When he awakened, night had plunged the jungle back into darkness. It was an almost absolute darkness. He couldn't even make out his hand. He shifted himself enough so that he could fall back into the grass bedding of the lean-to. He lay there tormented. He was wishing for rain, not for something to drink, but for a way to end his suffering from this utterly futile situation. He listened to the sounds of the forest, and wondered why no predator had come seeking an easy meal. *Maybe I reek so bad the stench is acting as a repellant.* He entered a state of reminiscence thinking first about Bernie, his long deceased first love. When his end came, would he see her again? He wondered if anyone even knew he was missing. He thought about Bernie's mother, Mary, the Ojibwa seer woman who had visions about things as they were happening. *Can Mary see me? Does she know I'm still alive? 'Does she know about what's happened to me? Can she see the condition I'm in? Christ, is she even still alive?* He knew they shared a connection based on things she'd told him in the past. The total darkness began to feel like a coffin. If it weren't for the unidentifiable sounds going on all around him, he thought, *this must be what it's like to be buried alive.*

He'd realized soon after he'd first regained consciousness that his captors had stripped him of everything but his fatigue shirt and pants. They'd taken his belt, his boots, he felt for his dog tags. They'd even stripped him of those. *Fuck, even if someone finds my remains, they won't be able to identify me. They won't know who I was.* He thought about how agonizing it must be for anyone to lose someone and not know what's become of that person. He knew the military didn't count a person dead unless they had an actual body, or damn certain proof of it. Not knowing how long he'd been a POW, he wondered if Leslie, and his mother had been notified he was missing. *Les, I'm here. I'm still alive. We both knew I might not make it home. I'm sorry. I'm sorry I'm still alive. I wasn't killed outright. It would be easier on you if I had been.* His thoughts shifted to his comrades. He hoped they'd made it. The weather had made it an extremely risky extraction. He felt feverish, parched and in terrible pain. *I think this is it. I don't think I can hang on. I'm so sorry you have to go through the pain of not knowing, Les.*

To his surprise he caught a brief flicker of light in the crypt of darkness surrounding him. He focused and a moment later there it was again. *Jesus, it's a damn lighten-*

ing bug? He hadn't seen lightening bugs during the entire time he'd been in country, but there was no mistaking it. He spotted three or four others. He lay back realizing the rain had ceased without his having noticed. He wondered if it was nearing the end of the rainy season. *Have I been missing that long?* Monsoon didn't usually end until early April. He slept.

Will awakened at first light. The rain still hadn't resumed. The light grew slowly in the jungle. He stripped some more seeds from the grass floor and ate them. He needed water. He scanned the area, but couldn't see standing water anywhere, no puddles, nothing. It occurred to him that there was a lot of moisture on the dense foliage surrounding him. Maybe he could find a way to capture some of it. He began dragging himself from the shelter. After a few feet, the broken cage he'd been confined to caught his eye. It was maybe ten feet away, but it took him an hour to reach it. *If I can salvage one of the longer bamboo sticks from it, maybe I can use it to get myself upright.* He was learning how to move himself so as to minimize the pain to his right shoulder, and broken leg. The cage side came apart easily. He used one of the vertical pieces to bring himself to an upright kneeling position, but without the use of his right hand and his weakened condition he was unable to achieve standing.

His frustration caused him to lash out in anger. He used the bamboo piece he was holding to bat at the cage that hung like a piñata. The pain he suffered wasn't worth the effort he'd made, but he made a discovery. Water splashed out from the top ends of the cage. He examined the pieces of the cage that were scattered on the ground. All but one of them had been cut so that there was at least four or five inches of hollow interior before a joint. He gathered each of the pieces and tried tossing them in the direction of the lean-to. He had several vessels he could use to collect water in if and when it rained. He felt heartened. Back at the lean-to he pushed each of the stalks into the ground. They'd act like rain gauges and collect water. He had three thick stalks and six thinner ones.

A desire to survive flickered. He remembered Thomas, Bernie's Ojibwa father. Thomas had given him a paw from an animal he'd trapped one winter. The animal had chewed it's paw off in order to escape the trap. It had sacrificed a part of itself in order to survive. He dragged himself toward the foliage that surrounded the small area of the encampment. The leaves of the foliage were wet with beaded droplets of water. Lying on his back. He reached up and with as much care as he could muster he folded one of the low hanging leaves. The water on the leaf rolled off the surface but he wasn't able to catch the few drops in his mouth. He held the leaf and tried shaking the surrounding foliage, several drops fell onto this crude funnel leaf. He was able to capture a few swallows that way. He searched for a broader leaf. He dragged himself around part of the perimeter of the encampment repeating this process until he'd managed to consume a few ounces of water. By late afternoon he'd made his way back into the lean-to and he ate some more grass seed. Out of sheer exhaustion he laid back and slept.

It was nearly dusk when it began raining lightly. He'd arranged his bamboo sticks in a vertical position near the lean-to. He was able to gather three or four more swallows of water before darkness enveloped him again. He lay in the lean-to listening to the rain and the forest. He knew he couldn't go on much longer like this. Without food he was losing even more strength. His leg was severely infected and oozing puss. *Christ, the infection may get me before starvation does.*

The rain increased, then stopped. It rained off-and-on throughout the night. He awakened once, but because of the totality of the darkness he didn't try to retrieve any of the water sticks'. Instead he used the leaf. By scooching his head and shoulders out of the lean-to, he was able to use the leaf to direct rain water into his mouth. He withdrew back under the shelter after slaking his thirst. Will knew he was running a fever. He began to shiver. He slept fitfully the rest of the night.

When morning came the rain had diminished to a drizzle. He drank again, this time using his sticks which were brimming over. He chewed more grass seeds. He realized that the seed supply was dwindling. Maybe he would be able to get another two or three day's 'meals' from this and the other lean-to. After that he'd be SOL. He decided to try again to work his way to a standing position. He got to a kneeling position and braced himself in a leaning position against one of the front uprights of the lean to. He rested for several minutes in that position to gather as much strength as possible before attempting to stand. Dreading the inevitable pain, he used the bamboo stick to steady himself and he worked his left leg into position to push up. He took two or three deep breaths and made a desperate effort. Pushing with his leg and pulling with his left arm he managed to slide up the bamboo upright to a standing position. He was trembling from the exertion. He wanted to scream out in triumph. The only sound he could produce was hoarse, raspy and painful. It felt like he had a strep throat. He was sweating, and tears cascaded down his cheeks, he was panting for breath.

Now-what? For that moment in time it didn't matter. He realized he was standing for perhaps the first time in maybe weeks. He gathered himself and cautiously pivoted himself around to lean his back against the upright. He considered trying to see if he could somehow hobble a few steps. It was impossible. He was too weak. He was beginning to tremble. He'd used up all of his energy. For the first time he realized how emaciated he was. He had no body-fat. He feared his muscles were beginning to atrophy. The trembling didn't cease. Having made a monumental effort to stand he didn't want to surrender his victory. Will stood for a while longer before trying to figure out a way to lower himself. He tried to pivot himself around to face the bamboo upright again. He had no strength left to support his body in making the effort. He lost his balance and was unable to prevent himself from falling. Upon impact with the ground a scorching explosion of pain ripped through him. He let out a barely audible scream of agony, then passed out.

Chapter 3

December 26th, 1967 was a bitter cold day. Thomas and Leslie, wearing snowshoes, were working Thomas's trap line. They'd started just before dawn. They were in a wooded area that offered them some moderate protection from the fierce northwest wind. It was about 8:30 in the morning and they'd completed about half of the line. As they approached one of the traps Thomas gasped, "Sweet Jesus."

"What is it, Thomas? What's wrong?" Leslie was startled by Thomas's alarmed expression.

The Indian moved cautiously up to the trap. He handed Leslie his rifle and stooped down to carefully release the jaws. He brought up a large bird. He stood up. "It's a red-tailed hawk." Thomas had an expression of terrible pain. "Leslie, there aren't any hawks around here this time of year. They've all migrated south." Thomas cradled the bird. "I don't understand."

"Is it alive, Thomas?" She didn't understand the reason for Thomas's concern.

He cautiously examined the bird. "Yes, but just barely." He looked up at her. "Leslie, we have to go. We have to get this bird home. I can come back later to finish the line."

Leslie carried both of their rifles. Thomas left the path of the trap line, taking a shorter route back to his truck. He had the hawk tucked inside his coat, with just its beak protruding. The snow was deep, even in the forest. When they came to an open meadow, the snow was drifted in places and it took real effort to climb over them. When they arrived at the truck Leslie stowed the rifles in the rack behind the seat. Thomas let her drive. En route to his house he murmured a low chant as if trying to appeal to the spirits. Neither of them spoke a word during the twenty minutes it took to get to his house.

Inside Mary met them in the kitchen as they entered the house. Her cheeks were wet with tears. She already knew what was happening. She told Leslie to call Augie and Jeanne to see if a messenger had come to the resort. Augie answered the phone. It still hadn't registered with Leslie that the injured hawk's discovery represented something ominous. She told him Mary had told her to call him. "What's wrong?" She told him about finding the hawk. "Oh my God," He sounded like he'd just been slapped. "Is it still alive? We'll be right there." He hung up abruptly.

Leslie turned to Mary who took hold of her hands. She took a deep breath. "Mary, is this about Will?"

Mary took Leslie in her arms. "Yes," Mary stroked her hair.

"What have you seen, Mary?" Mary seemed extremely reluctant.

Thomas cleared his throat and said softly, "Tell her, Mary. She needs to know."

Mary nodded, "Will's been captured. He's hurt very badly. He's still alive, but..." Mary stopped.

"But what, Mary?"

The tears were streaming down her face. Leslie wiped them away with her thumbs. "I don't know if he can survive what's happened to him. His spirit is struggling to decide whether to stay or go."

Leslie turned to Thomas. "Is what's happened to the hawk somehow connected to, Will?"

"I think so, Leslie."

"Are you saying the hawk's a kind of messenger?" Thomas nodded. "We have to try to save the hawk, don't we?"

Mary said, "I know this sounds crazy to you. Their spirits are connected in some way, Leslie. This wasn't an accident. If one of them dies so will the other."

Augie arrived several minutes later by himself. He came barging into the house. "I asked Jeanne to stay home just in case a message arrives."

Thomas had already found a large carton and he had the hawk lying on blankets in the box. Augie took his coat off. He bent over the bird examining it. Thomas told him, "its right leg is badly broken, and the right wing seems to be detached here at the shoulder. See the difference from the left one." Augie felt the shoulders. He agreed.

"How long do you think it was in the trap?" Augie asked.

"I ran the line early yesterday. It may have happened even late yesterday morning I don't know. Lucky no other animal found it." Thomas gently lifted one of the hawk's eyelids. "The bird needs fluids, Augie."

"We need to call Norma Gray."

"That's what I was thinking."

Augie got the phone book and began searching for her number. Leslie asked. "Who's Norma Gray?"

"She's a licensed wildlife rehabilitator." Thomas said. "Her full name is Norma Gray Eagle. I don't know of anyone more qualified to help than her. She's done amazing things with all sorts of animals. Raptors especially."

"What about the vet, Doug Kenyon?" Leslie asked.

"He's good," Thomas said. "If Norma thinks there's something Doug can do to help, she'll call him. They're friends. Doug isn't really supposed to treat wild animals. Norma can because she's Indian, and because she's licensed."

Augie was speaking with Norma. "Do you want one

of us to come get you? They've plowed the roads, but this wind is causing heavy drifting." When Augie hung up he reported. "She's going to drive over herself. She'll be here in a while. She told us to place the Hawk in a dimly lit, cool place. She said that it was important not to stress the bird. She's going to call Doug and see if he can meet her here. She agrees the bird needs fluids, and that's why she wants Doug."

"Let's move the hawk out to my workshop. It is cool and fairly dark." Mary told all three of them to go. She'd be okay by herself. Thomas picked the box up and the three of them went to the spacious workshop that extended off the rear of his garage.

The vet, Doug Kenyon arrived before Norma. He looked the bird over, but wanted to wait for Norma before doing anything. It took Norma well over an hour to get to Thomas's house. When she came into the workshop she said, "Augie was right, the roads are a bitch." Norma was a tall woman about the same height as Leslie, five eleven. She had a slender but muscular build, and graying hair pinned up loosely on the back of her head. She wore faded jeans, a turtleneck with a heavy plaid flannel shirt over it. She didn't wait for an introduction. She told Leslie who she was and they shook hands. Leslie felt an immediate confidence in her. Norma looked around Thomas's workshop. "Nice set up, Tommy," Leslie had never heard anyone call him anything but Thomas. Norma spotted the box. "Let's see what we've got here." She pulled out a pair of wire rim glasses and penlight from her shirt pocket.

She felt the bird all over finally placing her hand on its breast, holding it there for several moments. She stood up straight, placing one fist on her hip and pinching her lower lip. She wore a deep frowned expression. She walked across the workshop, pivoted and walked back. She did this three times before stopping at the box again. She looked directly at Thomas, “You know as well as I do that this is fucking nuts, Tom. I've never seen a hawk up here in the goddamn winter. Hawks aren't stupid. Why's it here? It's almost like it wanted to get caught.”

Thomas said nothing, he took Norma's arm, “Come on, Norma, I think you need to talk with Mary.” He led Norma back to the house. When they returned to the workshop several minutes later Thomas brought a percolator of coffee and mugs for everyone.

Norma pushed her sleeves up. She took Leslie's arm. “Come on girl. We've got some lives to try and save.” She turned to Doug, “I'm going to pull out some feathers here to expose a vein,” she pointed to the area. “I want you to set up a drip to get some fluid into this fellow?” Doug nodded. “Its right wing has been torn at the shoulder. Damned if I can figure out how that happened. I don't know if it can be fixed. We'll try. The leg is completely broken, and splinters of it are protruding. We need to pull it down first then, carefully try to put it back together. We'll put splints on all four sides of it to hold it in place. Even if it mends he might not have full use of those talons.” Norma stroked the bird. “It may be the cold temperatures are what's kept this young man alive.”

Norma had Leslie help her, instructing Leslie on what to do. The first task was to set up an IV to start hydrating the hawk. When Doug had contributed as much as he had to offer, he said he had to leave. “I'll stop by tomorrow to drop off another bag of fluid.” Everyone thanked him. He wished them good luck.

“We're down to that,” Norma muttered.

Norma and Leslie labored over the bird for nearly an hour before Norma declared “Okay, let's let this poor fellow get some rest. We're done for now.” It was mid-afternoon. Augie and Thomas had remained in the background watching what Norma was doing. They all retreated to the house. Norma went to the sink to wash her hands. "Hawk is unconscious. I wrapped him with gauze so he won't be able to thrash about when he regains consciousness. Tom, have you got any soft deer hide around?" He told her he did. Norma drew out a pattern on a paper grocery bag. "Cut out something like this. We need to make a hood for our friend. The hood will act as a blindfold and keep him from trying to fly. His being unconscious is working in our favor for right now, but if he doesn't come out of it pretty soon, like in the next day or so, he's probably not going to make it."

Thomas set to the task immediately. Norma took hold of Leslie's hands. "You were great today. I want you to know something. If that bird makes it, a large part of having saved his life will have come from you. I could feel it. Not many people have the gift of touch." Norma squeezed Leslie's arm. She then got a printed card out from one of her coat pockets. This is how you can reach me. I'll be back tomorrow if it doesn't snow another three fucking feet." Thomas appeared with the leather and the pattern drawn out on it. "Do you know how to put this on the hawk, Tom?" Thomas told her he thought he could figure it out. "Okay, if I were you, I'd put it on him as soon as you get done making it. If the bird regains consciousness, we don't want it to panic. We need to do everything we can to reduce as much stress as possible. It can kill him. He can't defend himself, and he doesn't know he's not in danger. He needs to become familiar with Leslie and learn to trust her."

Before leaving Norma asked if Thomas or Leslie had any questions. Leslie asked about food. Norma smiled. "Eating is a ways down on the list for right now sweetheart. We'll worry about that later."

Leslie accompanied Thomas out to his workshop. She watched him cut out the hood, slip it over the bird's head and tie it in place. He asked, "Have you ever heard of falconry, Leslie?"

"I've heard about it, but I don't know anything about it."

"Falconers use birds of prey to hunt with. They put a hood over the bird's head, just like this one so the bird won't take flight until a prey is spotted. Falconers wear a heavy leather glove called a gauntlet. The bird perches on the glove. When it comes time for the bird to go into action, the falconer removes the hood. When the hawk spots the prey, the falconer launches it, and the bird flies off to make the kill. The bird almost always stays atop the prey until the falconer retrieves it, and puts the hood back on. It's an amazing thing to watch, this relationship between man and bird."

Leslie showed a weak smile. "Thomas, what's amazing is what's happening. If Mary's right, it may mean something similar has happened to Will."

Thomas and Mary invited Leslie to stay with them for as long as needed. Thomas offered for her to stay in their deceased daughter's old room, but she wanted to be near the hawk. He set up a cot for her in the workshop. Before leaving to finish running his trap line he told her, "I'll be back before dark. Maybe someone from the Army will call to let you know what's happened to Will."

Mary and Leslie visited for an hour. Leslie made tea for the two of them and she brushed and combed Mary's long, almost white hair. Leslie asked about Norma Gray Eagle.

Mary smiled. "Norma's something else. We all went to school together. Norma was madly in love with Augie from grade school on. She was always kind of a Tomboy, like one-of-the-guys. When we got into high school Norma took to drinking. She only drank beer, but she drank a lot, and came to school either drunk or hung-over much of the time. Her mother died when she was only thirteen, and Norma's father ignored the kids. He'd take off and leave Norma and her older brother in charge of the younger ones, sometimes for several days. The rumor was that her older brother forced Norma to have sex with him frequently. That may be what got her started with drinking. The brother finally got into some serious trouble with the law, and the judge gave him a choice between joining the army, or going to prison. He chose the army, and he ended up going to Korea. He never came back." Mary sighed. "After her brother was killed, things got so bad for Norma and the kids the court came in and took custody of them and put them in foster homes. It could have gone either way for Norma, but she somehow managed to straighten herself out and she was finally able to get the kids back. She worked hard to keep a roof over their heads. I think Augie helped her out by giving her money from time to time. Augie and she have always been good friends. Norma never married. I don't really know how she got into working with injured animals. Taking care of them seems to have become her whole purpose in life. She has a gift for it. She's got her own place quite a ways out west of town. She's tough as a brick with most people, but she is one of the gentlest souls on earth with animals."

Mary took the hair brush from Leslie and had her sit on the floor so she could brush Leslie's hair. "I hope I don't upset you when I talk about Bernie." Leslie invited her to go ahead. "Bernie and I used to take turns doing one another's hair. It's one of the many things I miss about her." Mary went on about Norma. "I think Norma really likes you, Leslie. When I told her about what was happening, she just said that we needed to save this hawk. She goes around trying to give the impression she's really tough, but I think it's because she's afraid of being hurt."

"Do you think she's still in love with Augie?"

Mary stopped brushing Leslie's hair, and said softly, "Augie may be the only man on the face of the earth Norma has ever loved. She adores him to this day. I personally think that's why she moved out so far from town. She wanted to avoid running into him. She was shocked when she walked into the workshop and saw him standing there." Mary patted Leslie's head. "She did a good job of hiding her surprise."

"Does that mean she dislikes Jeanne?"

"No, I think she likes Jeanne, okay. She's come to accept nothing will ever happen between her and Augie. That doesn't change her feelings toward him though."

"Strange."

"How do you mean?" Mary asked.

"That's the way I felt about Will for a long time. I adored him, but I felt like he hardly knew I was alive. I'd gotten to where I was beginning to accept that was just the way it would always be. I knew I'd never love anyone the way I loved him." Leslie suddenly realized what she was saying. "Oh Mary, I'm sorry, I must sound like I was jealous of Bernie, and resented her."

"Shhhh," Mary quieted her. "We've talked about this before. She and Will were headed in different directions. It was just a matter of time before both of them turned around and faced that it was over between them. I know if Bernie was still alive she'd be pleased the two of you ended up together. You and Bernie are very different people, but you also had some things in common. I'm not offended. All of us love you, Leslie, and not just because you're with Will." "What I'm hearing is you're still not certain about Will's love for you. Trust me, Leslie, the love between the two of you is what's helping to keep him alive at this very moment."

Leslie turned to put her arms around Mary, "Is he

alive, Mary?"

"Yes," Mary paused. "Like the hawk, he's barely hanging on, but he's still alive." She went on, "There are some people looking for him. We can only hope they find him before it's too late. They're native people, and one of them has strong healing powers. Will has an ancient soul. He will benefit from the old ways this healer will offer him."

"I feel so helpless, Mary."

"I know. That's because you're not able to see the connection between what you and Norma are doing for the hawk, and Will's spirit." Mary patted Leslie's shoulder. "Norma's a gifted healer. She understands that finding the hawk wasn't an accident. She's aware of the link between the two of them." Mary looked serious. "I don't know how this story's going to end, Leslie. My seeing ability doesn't include fortune telling." Leslie chose not to challenge her last statement, but Mary had just predicted some friendly people were looking for Will.

Thomas came into the house. "I checked on the hawk before I came in. He seems about the same." He asked if Leslie had decided about staying. She said she thought she'd go back to the resort for tonight. She needed to get some things, but she'd be back early in the morning. "It's snowing again," Thomas informed her. "Call me in the morning if you need me to come get you."

Before leaving, Leslie went into the workshop to check the hawk. It lay very still, and she wondered if it was still alive. She touched it and could feel some warmth. She drove slowly on the way back to the resort. The snow had drifted in many places and she was glad to be driving Will's truck.

Chapter 4

Will opened his eyes, unable to focus at first. As his vision began to clear he saw he was not alone. Squatting directly in front of him was an almost elfin figure wearing a round straw hat and dark blue pants and shirt. The little man had a weathered, lined face, and a puggish little nose that angled upwards. His expression was impassive, but his eyes showed concern. The man was unarmed. He uncrossed his arms and reached out to touch Will. He placed his hand on Will's head, held it there for a few moments, then patted him gently. He turned his head and spoke over his shoulder to someone in a high-pitched voice that sounded rather sing-song. Soon someone handed the little man a small bowl. The little man slipped one hand behind Will's head and gently lifted. He brought the bowl to his lips and very slowly poured small amounts of a salty tasting liquid into his mouth. Will swallowed realizing how thirsty he was. When the bowl was empty the little man handed it to whoever was behind him. Will tried to turn his head to see who was off to the side. The movement brought intense pain. He vaguely remembered falling and wondered if he'd injured himself even more. The little man was handed another bowl.

He gave what sounded like a brief command, and almost instantly a much younger person appeared, knelt down and gently lifted Will's head. The little man dipped his fingers into the second bowl, and began feeding him. It looked like rice, but it had sweetness that reminded him of yams. The little man alternated back and forth between offering the liquid and the porridge-like concoction. Finally he stood, stepped back and very quickly several younger men stepped in. They placed what looked like a litter next to Will. Several hands slipped underneath him, and started to lift in unison. He experienced such excruciating pain in his right side, shoulder, and arm he tried to scream out. The group of men immediately ceased their effort, and at a command they stepped back. The litter was moved aside. The little man squatted next to him again. He studied Will before he proceeded to unbutton the front of his filthy, blood stained and mud caked fatigue shirt. He guided his fingers underneath the shirt slowly and diagnostically. Will winced as the hand neared his right shoulder. The little man guided his fingers downward and out. He stopped whenever Will flinched with pain. He finally gave another command and one of the young men unbuttoned Will's shirt entirely. He carefully pulled the shirt open. The little man leaned forward to look at Will's right shoulder. He began touching Will in various places. Will had suffered broken ribs when he was younger. The pain in his right side felt identical. Maybe they'd started to mend and he'd re-broken them when he fell. He didn't understand the severe pain in his shoulder. The little man finally stood and disappeared for several moments. When he returned he gave a command and another man held Will's head. The little man moved very quickly. He produced a devise that had two hollow reeds sticking out of a small ball-like thing. There was a single bamboo straw on the opposite side of the ball. He placed the two straws into Will's nostrils. He then blew a single sharp puff on the straw. Within seconds Will began to experience a warm glow that spread throughout his body. Moments later he felt completely relaxed like he was afloat in a dream state. Several hands raised Will's upper body. They removed his shirt and cut his encrusted t-shirt to remove it. He was conscious, and aware that he was being moved and manipulated, but oblivious to pain.

Once his upper body was fully exposed the little man squatted to examine Will again. When he spoke, Will assumed it was to inform his cohorts about his diagnosis. He gave instructions. Three of the men took a firm hold of Will. One held his neck, the other two held his left arm. The little man positioned himself on Will's right side. He placed a foot directly under his right arm and jerked hard on the arm. Will felt a sharp pop. The little man jumped quickly to a position behind Will and pushed on the back of Will's shoulder. He felt the shoulder carefully, before he began massaging it. Finally he raised Will's arm slowly, then brought it down to a perpendicular position. He moved it to the front, then back. When he was satisfied the 'operation' was successful. Will was lifted onto the litter. Within moments the entourage left the encampment, moving swiftly through the jungle. The litter bearers traded off at regular intervals. Each time they stopped to exchange bearers, the little man, or one of his apprentices fed Will a few swallows of the liquid. Every hour they would give him some of the other concoction. Whatever it was they'd given him previously to rid him of pain was repeated, but in smaller dosages so that he was able to be more aware of what was happening, without having to suffer the severe pain. They came to a stop at a place where Will heard what sounded like running water. He was stripped of the rest of his clothes. The group of men tending him seemed unperturbed by the wretchedness of his condition. They cleaned away the waste from his groin. He wouldn't be aware until later that, in the process of cleaning him patches of skin peeled off his buttocks, loins and genitals.

He was lifted and placed into a pool of water, where he was repeatedly bathed. Afterwards, he was patted dry and some sort of balm was applied. A warm poultice dressing was placed on his right side and to the area surrounding the protruding bone of his right leg. He was able to see where he'd been hit in the side by a bullet. Later, in reconstructing what happened the day he'd fallen from the helicopter; he'd concluded a bullet must have knocked the wind out of him and broken a couple of his ribs.

With his pants removed he was able to see the area surrounding the protruding bone. It was splintered and badly infected. He was amazed that it didn't seem to hurt. He didn't realize the lack of pain was a bad sign. He decided the little man who'd been treating his injuries wasn't an actual physician, but more of a medicine man.

Will was wrapped in a sarong and was given small portions of the tea, and the semi-solid mixture again and again. One man cleaned Will's teeth by rubbing them with a rough grass wrapped around his fore finger. He showed him how to do it himself. Darkness came. This strange little band of rescuers, all with their button noses, spoke very little, and only in soft, terse exchanges. They moved Will to a different location in the jungle away from the pond and the sound of rushing water. They were joined by a group of about a dozen others who were armed with M-16 rifles. Some had pineapple grenades. Will wondered, *Who are these people? Where did they get American weapons? Who sent them, or did they just happen upon me? Do any of them speak English? Where am I being taken? How far have we traveled? How far am I from where I was captured? How long have I been missing? What's the date?"*

It occurred to him that it hadn't rained the entire day. He wondered again if the monsoon season was over. Just before darkness fell, two of the little people appeared with what looked like a bed sheet and a small tube shaped pillow. They covered Will, and placed the pillow under his head. They spread similar cloths on the ground on either side of him, and lay down close to him and in a short time they were asleep. Once during the night the two night companions got up and helped Will to his feet. With a small dim lantern they led him to a place not far from the enclave. One of them demonstrated, by example, that this was the latrine area. Will urinated, but couldn't produce a bowel movement. He figured his guts were still trying to remember what food was.

As daylight began to creep into the jungle, Will awakened. His valets awakened with him. After he'd peed, one of them applied an ointment to his raw groin area again. Will felt an overwhelming sense of gratitude mixed with profound embarrassment. *Who are these people? How did they happen to find me? Had someone contracted with them and sent them on a search mission? Where are they taking me? They're armed, which means they're worried about encountering bad-guys.*

Despite the limited use of his right arm and hand he was now able to feed himself and drink. He continued to be brought the tea and the mixture throughout the next several days. As time passed his portions were increased and he was given some fruits. Some meat was eventually added to the mixture.

Not one of his rescuers spoke a word of English. However, they were masters of charade, and communicated with Will graphically using gestures of all sorts. The 'medicine man', massaged and manipulated his shoulder several times each day, extending its range of motion. He gave Will a cloth ball to squeeze to help him regain strength and use of his hand. A kind of temporary cast was fashioned for the broken leg using split bamboo. The brace could be removed in order to allow for cleansing the infected area and the application of poultices. The medicine man supervised the application of those four times each day. The man's expression never changed except for a slight glimmer of brightness in his eyes that Will interpreted as approval.

Early one morning a slight young man came rushing into the encampment delivering a message to the medicine man and two of the others. After a brief exchange, a directive was given, and within minutes the entire group was ready to go. Will had been given a bamboo crutch a couple of days before. He'd been using it to make short trips to the latrine. He was placed on the litter again and strapped down.

Although there had been no show of alarm, he sensed from the haste of the evacuation they were in some kind of danger. Before long they started moving up into more rocky and steeper terrain. The armed men dropped back covering the rear of the procession. By late morning Will realized they were ascending a mountain. It was requiring all of the men to carry the litter up the increasingly steeper jagged incline. In places they needed to use ropes to hoist him. The foliage was disappearing. Will caught glimpses of the jungles below, an endless panorama of various greens that rolled and undulated as far as the eye could see. There were a few puffs of cumulus clouds, but otherwise, the sky was clear. He'd only seen moments of blue sky over the past five or six months.

By evening they reached a sort of broad ledge on the side of the mountain. The mountain extended higher. There was a fairly large cavernous opening and several people came out to greet the team of rescuers, if that's what they were. Several women and a few small children were among them. There was soft chatter. He was escorted to a latrine area that was shared by both sexes. He was self conscious about using it in the presence of women.

That night he was taken into the cave. There were a

few small fires burning. Will ate the first hot meal he'd consumed since before leaving on patrol before Christmas, however long ago that had been. He watched the surrounding people. Many of the couples chatted quietly with one another, and he saw exchanges of affection. He thought about him and Leslie. *She must know by now I'm MIA.* He was surrounded by fifty or more people gathered in this cave. They had shown him nothing but kindness. He felt like an alien unable to communicate to share any of his thoughts or feelings with any of them.

He'd become familiar with a few individuals. Despite the language barrier, he'd learned some of their names. They, on the other hand, could not say his name to save their souls. He wondered if they simply couldn't hear the 'L' or the R' sound. Maybe those sounds were absent from their language.

The wound to his side was beginning to heal. The leg was another matter. He was becoming increasingly concerned about gangrene setting in. He feared that it might end up needing to be amputated despite the medicine's man repertoire of healing tricks. He tried not to dwell on it. He made every effort to remind himself he was lucky to still be alive at this point. If he ended up losing a leg in the process, that was a small price to pay. He wondered if anyone in the outside world was aware he was still alive.

As the days passed Will realized he was beginning to regain some strength and stamina. He was able to move around with the use of his crutch and he was getting feeling and movement back in the fingers of his right hand. He found a relatively smooth small rock he used to do exercises. He did curls to strengthen his biceps and arm raises to strengthen his shoulder. The right shoulder was still very tender. He could not lie on his right side at night. He experienced so much pain when he changed positions while sleeping, it awakened him.

To his surprise the apparent leader of this group of people, a man named Phong Dieu, presented Will with his fatigue shirt and pants. They were clean, and smelled fresh. They'd also been mended. The right pant leg had been shortened to just below the knee. With help he abandoned his sarong and put on his uniform. He was handed a small mirror. He was astounded to see himself. His beard was six inches long, light brown and shaggy. His hair was past his ears and scuffled. *I look like a wild man,* he thought to himself. One of the men took several pictures of him with an old accordion-type of camera. He shocked Will when he handed him three photos that had been taken of him when he'd first been discovered. Will gasped at the horrible sight of himself. He was unrecognizable. He covered his mouth and tried to choke back tears. 'Oh my god, Oh my god, Oh Jesus'. The photographer touched his arm and repeated a phrase several times. Will had no idea what the man was saying to him, but the gentle consoling tone spoke for itself. He motioned to Will the photographs were for him to keep. Will wanted to destroy them. Using pantomime, the man let Will know he'd be given copies of the pictures he'd just taken.

Will asked himself. *Why the hell are they even taking pictures of me? What purpose can these possibly serve?* The most promising scenario was that they'd end up in American hands. Perhaps they'd be given to another LRRP team, or some CIA operatives. It was common knowledge the CIA had agents working with Laotian and Cambodian guerrilla units in areas close to their borders with Vietnam.

Another puzzle was the drums. He would hear the beat of a distant drum, then one closer, then one very close by. It went beyond this mountain up and down the line. He concluded it was a method of communication like Morse code? *Christ, this is right out of an old western movie, the Indians communicating with other bands of Indians.*

It was apparent these people were not from here. They'd fled from somewhere else and were here seeking refuge. They'd cleverly 'taken the high ground' thinking it was more defensible. It would be if Charlie was stupid enough to launch a frontal assault. The VC were more likely to resort to attrition by waiting and starving them out. These people didn't seem to realize they'd put themselves in a position of being trapped and under siege. The VC would begin sending snipers on a regular basis to pick off a few of them. Amazingly, small groups of men arrived a couple of times a week carrying supplies. God only knew how they'd been able to find their way here undetected. Evidently there was a source of water. Will thought they were too high up for there to be springs. Maybe it was rain water that was migrating down through fissures in the bedrock. If monsoon season was over, it meant the water supply would be coming to an eventual end, then what?

It rained occasionally now. Sometimes it would last for two or three hours and the women would make the most of it by doing laundry. Everything in the encampment was well organized and nothing was wasted. Like the native Americans, these people were in tune with nature and they appeared to know how to 'live off the land'.

One day Phong Dieu led Will deep into the cave. He showed him two cases of rifles, a cache of ammunition and some boxes of grenades. There were no other weapons. He handed Will one of the rifles, a cloth bag with half-a-dozen clips of ammunition and a few grenades. They nodded to one another. Will interpreted it to mean, he'd just been recruited and was now one of them.

Late that same afternoon a young messenger arrived. After a brief exchange Phong Dieu issued some orders and in less than a minute several armed men gathered around him. He spoke briefly, and the men dispersed heading down the mountain in pairs, going off in different directions. Just as quickly, women began putting out the cooking fires, and gathering pots, bowls, and cooking utensils. Will approached Phong Dieu who was standing near the edge of the precipice surveying the mountain below. He heard the drummer begin to beat out a message, perhaps of alarm, although he maintained a distinct unhurried beat as if to enunciate clearly. Will addressed Phong Dieu pointing down the mountain, he said VC several times. Phong Dieu didn't understand. "Vietcong?" Will asked.

Phong repeated, "Vietcong," shaking his head yes.

Will hobbled to the other side of the precipice. Phong Dieu stood watching. Using a burnt stick from a nearby fire Will drew a picture of the cliff. With gestures he tried to communicate to Phong Dieu that the sides of the ledge needed to be protected as well. After two or three tries Phong Dieu seemed to grasp what Will was trying to convey. He walked quickly to one side of the ledge, then to the other. *Does he understand, they need to protect their flanks on both sides?*

Phong Dieu went into the cave and returned with a young woman carrying a rifle with a bag of ammunition slung over her shoulder. He gave her some instructions and it became obvious she'd been assigned to lead Will to some place in particular. She took his rifle and ammunition and patiently began to lead the way. Will looked back to see Phong Dieu heading in the opposite direction. He followed her hobbling along a circuitous path that led downward from the left side of the ledge. Half an hour later they arrived at a jumble of boulders. They worked their way from one to another and she assisted him in getting atop one of the largest ones. Will was panting from the effort. She had what looked like a bota and she handed it to him. He expected it to be water but instead it turned out to be a broth flavored with strong spices. She smiled at his surprised expression.

They took up watch together, but after a while Will's leg began to throb. He tried rubbing it hoping it was just the result of overexertion, but it kept getting worse. On top of it he had to pee. He nudged her and pointed to his leg, and at the same time he grimaced, he was in pain. She nodded, crept off the boulder and disappeared. He rolled to his side, unbuttoned his fly and relieved himself. He tried to resume guard duty, but the pain was getting worse by the minute. Evening was approaching. He knew it would be dark in another hour. It was already starting to cool off. Nighttime on the mountain could get quite cool.

Just when he didn't think he could last one more minute, the woman returned. She was accompanied by the medicine man who surprised Will. He didn't even bother to look at Will's leg. Instead he began probing his trapezius muscles. When he found a spot that caused Will to flinch, he gently manipulated the area, and within moments the pain began to subside. He demonstrated what he'd done to the girl. He looked at Will's leg, applied some more poultices and patted him before leaving.

Before long darkness enveloped the mountain. They could barely even see one another, let alone any movement from below. They sipped some more broth and covered themselves with the light blankets she'd brought with her. They had to rely exclusively on listening for any sound or movement. Will had to remind himself it was just as dark for Charlie. He couldn't fathom anyone being able to traverse this rough terrain in such darkness.

Chapter 5

When Leslie got to the resort she was glad to see Feisty's car. His real name was Francis Noonan. Will and he had become close friends years before and Will had given him the nickname of Feisty because it matched his scrappy character. He and his wife Sunny were living in Chicago at the present time while Feisty completed his architectural internship. Sunny was an Ojibwa Indian who'd grown up on the nearby reservation. They'd driven up to spend Christmas at the resort and had arrived just minutes before Leslie got there. Feisty gave Leslie a long hug telling her Augie had just given them the news about Will. "I don't know what to say, Leslie. I wonder if the Army even knows Will's missing. I mean, you'd think they'd have notified you by now if they did." She agreed. "I'm pissed with this stupid war. If Will was here right now, I'd chloroform him, throw him in the trunk and haul him off to Canada."

"I'd help you."

As soon as Leslie got her coat off, Jeanne handed her a glass of wine. Feisty and Sunny were beer drinkers and had already opened a couple of bottles. Augie asked Leslie how the hawk was doing.

"It seems to be about the same." She went to stand in front of the fire. "I'm really impressed with Norma."

"She's an amazing lady," Augie said. "She has a rare gift. It took her a long time to discover that about herself."

Jeanne smiled at Augie. "Norma's had the hots for you since kindergarten."

"The woman's got good taste."

Sunny, had finished nurse's training three years ago. She was working at one of the large hospitals on Chicago's south side, near where she and Feisty lived. She asked Leslie some questions about what Norma was doing for the hawk. Sunny knew Norma, and that Norma was a licensed wildlife rehabilitator. Leslie told them how Thomas and she had come upon the hawk that morning. "Thomas immediately sensed it had some meaning and it was critical we get help for it. We dropped everything and took off for his place. I think he knew it was a sign of something but he didn't say what. Of course, when we got there, Mary already knew what had happened. She affirmed what Thomas suspected." Leslie described the hawk's injuries and what Norma and the vet were doing to treat it. Sunny asked if she could come to see the hawk tomorrow. Leslie hesitated telling her what Norma said about trying to avoid stressing the bird.

Augie had been quiet. He got up to mix himself another drink, something he seldom did anymore. Jeanne watched him with concern. She knew he and Thomas had been taken captive for a brief time when they'd been in Korea. It had happened when Chinese forces stormed into North Korea to prevent the retreating North Korean army from being overrun and defeated.

Augie shook his head. "I can't believe this is happening. If Will has the same injuries as the hawk and he's alone, I don't know how he'll be able to survive. The enemy's not going to care for him."

Leslie stepped in, "Mary says Will's badly hurt, but he's still alive. She's worried that his spirit is very weak. I get the feeling she sees the hawk as more than just a messenger. She didn't come right out and say it, but I sense she feels Will and the hawk are somehow connected and share the same spirit. If one dies, the other one will, too. She seems to feel, if we can save the hawk, he'll survive."

No one ever questioned the veracity of Mary's visions, but some of her interpretations of them seemed far-fetched at times. Out of their love and respect for her no one was willing to challenge her take on what was happening now.

Jeanne got up and went to Augie. He set his drink down on the counter and put his arms around her. "Will's kind of our son. We've both felt that way about him almost from the start." They held one another for a long while. "I guess I've never really considered what my parents went through when Thomas and I were in Korea. They loved Thomas as much as they did me. They must have suffered terribly. They never said so, but I sensed something different in them when we returned home. It was like they were unsure of how to treat us, afraid they'd say or do the wrong thing. I remember saying to my mother, 'Mom it's me. This is Thomas, remember'?"

"How did she react?"

"She started to cry, and said, 'I know, but neither of you are the same. You went away boys, you've come home old men. That war did something to both of you. It's almost like you're visitors. We only know a part of you. There's another part we'll never know. All we're left with is the memories of who you were."

"Was she right?"

"Probably," Augie said. "I think we all finally came to accept that none of our lives would ever be the same again. I think they came to understand that Thomas and I had been through some things that no one could understand, not unless they'd been through it themselves. They learned to let it be, but it saddened them."

The others had been listening. Feisty said, "You're

saying that if Will makes it back, he's not going to be the same person we knew."

"Count on it."

"Is that why you left here and moved to the city?" Jeanne asked.

"I don't know. I just knew things had changed for me and I felt I had to get out of here. I didn't know what the hell I wanted."

"What about Thomas, what did he do?"

"He drank himself to oblivion for a long time. He couldn't escape into the white man's world, so he just tried to escape the world period."

"Does anyone ever get over those kinds of experiences?" Leslie asked.

"I've thought about that a lot over the years, Leslie." Augie sipped some more of his drink. "I don't think it ever goes away. Time's not the great healer it's cracked up to be. What happens is, over time the memories occur less often, they become less intense, and even less painful. Time doesn't do that by itself. Each of us has to decide not to allow that stuff to dominate our lives. It's not like a person can just say to themselves, 'Okay, that's enough, I'm turning this off '. It doesn't work that way. I guess it's a lot like having to cope with an addiction. It's learning to accept that you're stuck with something that you're going to have to deal with for the rest of your life."

"So what's it like for you now, Augie?" Feisty asked. "Do you still have times when the stuff you went through in Korea comes back to bite you?"

"Yeah, it still does from time to time. The crazy thing is I never know when. I mean the memories aren't tied to anniversary dates, or a gun goes off, or a headline in a newspaper. It just happens unexpectedly. I'm sick about whatever's happening with Will right now. I am worried about how it's going to affect him if he survives."

"You know what, Augie? Will's a sensitive guy. Sometimes, too sensitive, but he's tough. He's a survivor. I've got a feelin' he's gonna make it." Feisty put a hand on Leslie's shoulder." I mean it, Leslie."

"Thanks Feisty." They hugged one another.

The next morning was sunny, but extremely cold with temperatures in the minus teens. The wind had finally died off during the night. Leslie had stayed in the guest bedroom at Augie and Jeanne's. She was up early and made coffee. She wanted to go to Thomas and Mary's right away. She needed to stop at August Loon to get the things she needed to take with her. She was startled when the phone rang. It was Feisty. "We're up and wondered if you wanted to stop for some breakfast.

Leslie invited them to come over to the resort instead. Feisty said they'd be there in a few minutes. When they arrived, Feisty sent Sunny in while he started the engine on Will's truck. He came into the house as Jeanne entered the kitchen. "Christ, it's cold. I had a tough time getting Will's truck started." Leslie reported the temperature at twelve below.

Augie entered the kitchen and greeted everyone as he poured himself some coffee. He took a chance and called Thomas knowing he might have left earlier to run his trap line. To his surprise Thomas picked up the phone in his workshop.

"How's the hawk doing?"

He reported things were about the same. "As soon as Leslie gets here, I'm going out to pull all of my traps." Augie offered to go with him. Thomas gave a slight laugh. "You're in no shape to be trudging around in deep snow, Augie. Thanks anyway. Norma called and said she'd be here around ten to check on the hawk."

Augie asked, "Does she need some money?"

"Norma always needs money, Augie. The problem is, she spends almost everything she makes on the animals she's caring for. If you're concerned about what she needs for herself, then you need to have it delivered anonymously. If you take it to her yourself, she'll be offended and think you're treating her like a charity case, which, of course, she is."

"I understand," Augie said. "I'll ask Jeanne to put together a list of things?"

After breakfast Feisty and Sunny started carrying in a supply of firewood. Leslie left for Mary and Thomas's.

A soldier came to Augie and Jeanne's house that afternoon with the announcement that, "First Lieutenant Willis Morrissey was reported as missing in action on the 24th day of December 1967." The notification had no details about what had occurred other than to say witnesses had reason to believe Lieutenant Morrissey had been taken captive by enemy forces. The military wished to assure the family every effort was being made to try to 'secure the safe release of Lieutenant Morrissey'.

Leslie called Will's mother to inform her of the official news. Helen was so distraught she told Leslie she couldn't talk right now. When she called Leslie later that evening the two of them talked for over an hour.

Weeks went by with no word about Will. Mary seemed sure he was alive, but she said she didn't know what kind of shape he was in. Everyone suspected she was trying to spare them from the truth of what she saw. Then one morning in early April, Mary and Leslie were having some mid-morning tea. Mary suddenly held up her hand. "Leslie, it's the hawk. I think it's coming out of its slumber."

Leslie jumped up and started for the workshop. She stopped. "I need to call Norma."

"See if its eyes are open first," Mary advised. Leslie came back into the house a short time later reporting it was awake." Did you put the hood back on?" Mary asked.

"Yes," She picked up the phone to call Norma. Norma answered about the fifth ring, sounding a bit winded. Leslie told her the news. Norma said she'd be there as soon as she could, which she warned might be over an hour. Leslie asked if she should call the vet Doug Kenyon. Norma told her to hold off, they'd decide after Norma had seen the bird.

Norma arrived at Thomas's in a little less than two hours. She looked perturbed. "The goddamn transmission in that old truck is fucked-up. I had to keep it in low gear all the way here. Leslie thought about lending her Will's jeep. "Where's Tom?" Norma asked. Leslie told her he was at the resort. He and Augie were in the process of getting the resort ready to reopen for another season. "Jesus Christ, what's that damn fool Indian doing still working his ass off for Augie?" Leslie was amused that Norma called Thomas an Indian being one herself.

"They're friends. It gives them both something to do. They'd probably drive both of their wives crazy if they were around all the time."

Norma offered a rare apology. "You're right, Leslie. They're both good men, neither of them are lazy." She carefully lifted the hawk out of the box. Leslie untied the hood and slipped it off. Norma smiled. "Look how quickly the pupils adjust to the light," she said as she held the bird admiringly. She spoke in a soft tone," What a handsome fellow you are." She looked at Leslie, "He's a mature hawk. He's probably about four or five years old. You can tell by the feather markings and the color of his beak." She gently touched it's beak and the hawk opened it part way. "Are you hungry? I'll bet you'd love a nice chunk of raw meat."

Leslie asked Norma if she should see if Mary had any thawed meat. Leslie started for the house. "If Mary doesn't have any thawed out, I'll run into town to get some." Leslie returned a few minutes later with some leftover cooked meat.

Norma frowned. "We can try it. I don't know if he'll take it cooked. To Norma's surprise he did. She looked at Leslie, "I don't mean to be holding out false hope, but if Mary's right, it could mean someone's caring for Will right now." She switched to another topic. "There's no way to really prevent a wild animal from imprinting on the human who cares for it. The primary way they imprint is through what they see as their source of food. You're it. He sees you as his care giver" Norma explained a lot of dos and don'ts in handling the bird. "Things are looking pretty good, Leslie. I wouldn't have bet a slug this guy was going to make it when I first saw him."

Leslie said, "You looked like you were really debating what to do."

Norma looked at her. "I'll be honest with you. Until I talked with Mary, I really thought the best thing would be to have Doug end the bird's suffering. We took a gamble, and it looks like it's paying off. "I don't know if the hawk's progress is a sign that Will's healing. If Mary's right, maybe their spirits are connected and they're working to help heal one another. Who knows." Norma returned to the practical. "One of the things we have to be concerned with from now on is reintroducing him to the wild. He needs to spend increasing amounts of time outside. We need to extend the time he can stand on his own. We'll set up a log for him outside where he can perch. Hawks prefer being able to perch up high where they can spot prey, but this fellow's not ready to fly yet.

"Norma, how did you learn all of this stuff?"

"Observation and having lived close to nature all my life. I learn things every day from the creatures themselves. Don't think I haven't screwed-up and lost some of them. Christ, I've lost lots of them. I guess some of it's just plain good old common sense, some of it's dumb luck, some of it's a gift and a lot of it is hard work and a willingness to risk yourself."

"Do you ever take apprentices?"

Norma's expression, which was usually hard and serious, softened. "I never have, Leslie, but I think I'd be willing to make an exception with you." She started for the door. "You seem to have the gift, and you have a gentle soul."

Over the next two weeks the hawk continued to improve. It was able to stand on both feet, but could only flex its talons slightly. Norma had Leslie work at stretching those tendons. The hawk's diet progressed from ground meat to chunks of chicken, sometimes rabbit. He trusted Leslie enough to allow her to carry him on her gauntlet covered arm. He'd make a screeching sound whenever she appeared. He also screeched when he needed to be taken out to eliminate. After two more weeks Norma removed the gauze binding that had served as a kind of straight-jacket, preventing the hawk from trying to flap it's wings. The hawk tried to stretch both of them out. He could barely move the right one. Norma showed Leslie how to manipulate and massage the shoulder area. She cautioned Leslie not to take the bird outside untethered. "If he manages to get airborne, he may injure himself all over again. He doesn't have the strength to sustain flight yet. Maybe he never will. We'll just have to wait to see."

By late April Leslie was able to take the hawk with her when she went to Norma's place. Norma always welcomed her and the two would spend hours together, Norma showing her what to do with various animals. Augie was curious about the relationship that was developing between them. He remarked to Jeanne, "Norma's always been kind of a loner. I wouldn't say she's shy. She's just not what you'd call very sociable. She guards her privacy. I think she trusts the animals she works with more than most people. I'm surprised she's opened up to Leslie. They seem to be developing a friendship."

Leslie decided to name the hawk Merlin. Over-shadowing the joy of seeing it's progress was not knowing anything about Will except for what Mary reported. She was of the opinion he'd been abandoned by his captors, but she either couldn't or wouldn't say what kind of shape he was in. A few days later she told Thomas Will had been found by some native people and a very powerful medicine man was caring for him. Thomas expected her to be pleased that Will was finally safe and in good hands. Instead she warned that all of them were in jeopardy, they were one step ahead of an enemy and they were fleeing for their lives. During the next several days Mary seemed perplexed. She admitted she didn't know what was going on. She thought Will was still alive, but something was interfering with her being able to see. She told Thomas she was fearful that something had happened to Will's vision. Thomas seemed surprised and he asked, "Are you saying you see through others? If they lose their ability to see, then you can't either?" She shrugged. "Are you sure? Are you just discovering this now?"

"Thomas, you know I've never questioned my ability as a seer for fear of losing the gift. I don't know what's going on. I'm just guessing. Maybe I'm all wrong. I'm sorry."

Thomas knew that Mary's ability didn't extend to everybody. It was limited to the special few she felt connected to. He also knew she couldn't force it to happen. 'It just did'. "What if Will was knocked unconscious? I mean there was a period of time after he first disappeared that you weren't able to see what was going on with him. You thought he was disoriented and in and out of a coma for the next several weeks." She agreed that was a possibility. They both resigned themselves to having to wait to see. It was what it was.

Chapter 6

Will guessed it was somewhere around 10:00 o'clock when the three-quarters waning moon began to rise. The sky was fairly clear with just a few tufts of clouds. A mist hung over the jungle below. After spending months sweating in the jungles, the cooler nighttime mountain air felt almost frigid. An hour passed before the sound of rifle fire erupted. It sounded like M-16s. It was a brief volley, then silence again. It didn't sound close, nor did it sound like there had been return fire. Another hour passed. His leg was beginning to throb again. He touched the woman and pointed to his leg. Just as she was about to begin massaging his neck, as the medicine man had shown her, there was a movement below and to their left. Will carefully brought his rifle up in front of him, and he crept closer to the edge. There was just enough light from the moon for him to make out two figures picking their way cautiously up the rocky mountain side. They were thirty yards below garbed in dark clothing. He brought the rifle to bear, but he couldn't get a clear sighting. He didn't want to shoot and miss. It would give their position away. The woman moved into position next to him.

Will reflected back to the unit he'd been operating with at the time of his capture. They'd trained and developed tactics for handling situations just like this. Each man knew what target to select so no two of them had the same one. They couldn't allow either of these guys to escape. He had no idea about how good a marksman the woman was. He'd try to get both of them.

They suddenly disappeared from sight. Moments

later one of them appeared on a large flat boulder below. He'd been boosted up on the rock by his colleague. He reached down to help the other one up. A moment later, both men were standing atop the rock. Will decided to switch to full automatic. Before he could take aim the woman fired four quick rounds. The impact of the bullets knocked both men off the boulder. She and Will lay motionless on the ledge listening for any movement. Several minutes went by, then the young woman got up and scrambled down the hillside. She returned ten minutes later carrying two AK-47s and a bag of clips. It wouldn't be until the next day he'd discover she'd also cut an ear off of each one of them. He wondered if it was a way of keeping a body count or was it a trophy.

Gunshots sounded from the direction they heard before. This time the higher pitched sound of M-16s, were answered by the louder thudding sound of AK-47s. The shooting continued. *Charlie's launching an assault. They've got their weapons on full automatic. They're probably hoping to terrify and over-run our guys.* Will listened trying to figure out what was happening. He'd allowed his attention to be diverted away from keeping watch. The woman raised up. Will looked to see she was taking aim. Two dark figures were scampering across the rocks fifteen feet below them. Before he could bring his weapon to bear she opened fire. Both figures dropped. One of them appeared to be dead, but the other one was trying to drag himself toward cover. She leapt up and deftly jumped from boulder to boulder in pursuit of him. When she returned she was slightly out of breath. He assumed she'd finished the job but he hadn't heard a shot fired. She removed the clip from her rifle, put in a fully loaded one and handed Will the one remaining round left from the first clip.

He stuck the bullet in his shirt pocket. He'd keep it

as a talisman. They resumed their vigil. The shooting they'd heard earlier had ceased entirely.

Will dozed off for an hour. When he awakened he discovered he'd been covered with two additional blankets, and the woman offered him some lukewarm tea. They took turns keeping watch until dawn. There were no more exchanges of gunfire the rest of the night. As the sky lightened, it looked like it would be a clear day. The jungle below was completely enveloped in a dense, cloud-like fog. Will thought it was exquisite. *No one looking at a picture of this seemingly tranquil scene would ever guess men were trying to kill one another here.* It seemed surreal and incongruous.

Before the sun began to appear above the horizon, two young men arrived to replace Will and the woman. He was stiff and his leg was throbbing. She helped him back to the cavern where the medicine man was waiting to take care of him. A distant drum sounded. When it stopped, the drum messenger above the caves repeated the message as if forwarding it down the line. The message sending went back and fourth for fifteen minutes and Phong Dieu and his lieutenants listened intently.

Fires had been started, and food was being prepared. Phong Dieu and the woman Will had stood guard with, motioned for him to join them. The three of them sat together just outside the cavern entrance. Phong Dieu and the woman carried on a conversation with one another. She gestured toward Will a couple of times. Finally, Phong Dieu reached over and took Will's hand and shook it as he repeated the same phrase several times. Will decided he was being thanked for last night. After they'd eaten, Phong Dieu escorted Will inside the cave and led him to a sleeping area. He was asleep within minutes.

He was awakened when the drummer above the cave began beating a frantic alarm. He struggled to his feet. The pain in his leg was so severe he stood immobilized waiting for it to subside enough for him to hobble. Women and children were scurrying to get deeper into the cave. He managed to get a young boy to hand him his rifle and the bag of clips. By the time he got to the cave entrance the drumming had ceased. There were six armed teenage boys stationed along the ledge in front of the cave. He had to get off his feet. He managed to lie down and elevate his leg on a boulder. The pain gradually lessened enough for him to roll onto his stomach and begin crawling toward the far left side of the cliff. Two of the boys left their posts to help him, dragging him carefully to where he could see the trail. After they got Will into a sitting position with his back to a rock, one of them left and went into the cave. The other brought him some water. The escapement was in the shade. Will concluded the cave entrance must be facing easterly and it was mid-afternoon. The boy who'd gone in the cave returned with the medicine man. The old man lifted Will's pant leg to examine the infected area. He reached into his bag and produced what looked like a bay leaf. He pantomimed for Will to chew on the leaf and swallow the juices. Minutes later Will began to feel a euphoric relief from all of his pain. *Christ, I haven't felt this pain free since I was ten years old.* He was amazed. He was aware of everything going on around him. He felt like he could get up and make his way down the mountain to where he'd been last night. The medicine man must have anticipated his reaction. The man ran his fingers over Will's right thigh and Will found the leg wouldn't work. So much for trying to go anywhere. The man reached into a lidded jar and pulled out what looked like rice which he put on the infected area. Will would learn later it wasn't rice, but maggots. The fly larvae were eating the bacteria that were causing his infection.

When the medicine man was finished he got up from

his squatting position and went back into the cave. Will didn't like where he'd been placed. He couldn't see much of the trail he was trying to guard. He got the attention of one of the boys who'd helped him before. The young man helped him to his feet and a few yards down the trail where he could take in much more of what lay below. He was also able to sit. He checked his weapon and set a couple of clips on the rock next to him. He was about to settle back and wait, when he spotted some peripheral movement among the rocks to his left. He scanned the terrain carefully finally spotting two figures making their way up the mountain. They must have figured out where Phong Dieu and his men were guarding the trail and they'd taken an arduous detour to get around them. It looked like they were headed for the cave itself rather than attempting a flank attack on Phong Dieu's position from behind. They disappeared behind an outcropping of rocks for a few moments. Will changed his position, switched his rifle to automatic and waited for them to reappear. When they did he opened fire killing both of them.

Several VC emerged from the sparse jungle below. They apparently thought the shots had come from the infiltrators at the cave. They started up the trail moving swiftly, intent on getting to the cave. Will was in a good position to block anyone who might get past Phong Dieu and his men but he kept a watchful eye out for anyone else avoiding the trail. Shooting erupted further down the mountain and lasted for several minutes. After it stopped he spotted Phong Dieu coming up the trail by himself. He had a grim expression. He helped Will back up the trail.

When they arrived at the cave, the medicine man was waiting. He immediately began attending Will's leg. Phong Dieu and the Medicine man spoke in low tones. They seemed to be discussing their situation.

No more shots were fired the rest of the day. Will and Phong Dieu both retreated to the cooler interior of the cave, and slept until evening. They awakened to the sound of the drum. Phong Dieu listened, then sent a courier with a message to be sent by the drummer. Minutes later the drummer started telegraphing. Will sat up dreading the excruciating pain he knew was coming the moment he stood. It always took several minutes for the pain to subside enough for him to move about.

He wondered if anyone had discovered the bodies of the two VC he'd shot earlier. His mind segued to the first time he'd shot one of the enemy. It was before he'd become a LRRP. He was in charge of a platoon that was on a routine patrol. They'd entered a small village where they discovered a tunnel entrance under a grass mat in one of the hooches. They tossed several tear gas canisters into the tunnel and waited to see what happened. Charlie always had alternative exits to their tunnels. Will and another man had taken a position at the edge of a nearby rice paddy. Several minutes later three VC came crawling out of an opening into the dry paddy. One of them raised his weapon to shoot. Will emptied a clip into the man. The other two were caught in a volley of automatic fire from others in the unit. Will went behind an oxcart, vomited and began to tremble. His sergeant, who was on his third tour, led him behind a hut, lit a cigarette and handed it to Will." It's nothin' to be ashamed about, LT. I felt the same way the first time I killed one. I'd be worried about you if you felt nothing or you'd enjoyed it. You did what you had to do. Charlie would have greased your ass if you hadn't beaten him to the draw. It gets easier. You done good." The sergeant lit a cigarette off the one he'd just finished. He left Will and went to assemble the men. He assigned a couple of point guards and they left the village.

The sergeant had been right. 'Killing had gotten easier'. Since having been taken captive, and left to die such a merciless death, things had changed for Will. He had no compunction about killing VC. He felt a loyalty to these people who'd saved him. He wanted to do whatever he could to help them survive. When he'd first arrived in Vietnam he'd been a determined, gung-ho soldier 'out to win the war'. He soon began to see the situation as hopeless. An American victory was impossible. The whole thing was an exercise in futility. The idealistic part of him gave way to cynicism and anger. He just wanted to complete his tour, finish his military obligation and return to the world he'd left behind. He knew being here had changed him, but he had no idea the challenges he'd face later on in trying to rebuild his life.

The medicine man appeared and gave Will another one of the leaves. He cleaned the infected area and applied more of what Will thought was rice while waiting for the juices to take effect and bring relief. He wondered why the man didn't give him a snort of the stuff he'd used before to knocked him out, and just cut the leg off. Will was resigned to the eventuality of losing it. *Why wait? Why not just get it over with and move on?*

The answer to that question began to unfold. Will noticed several things. The women in the encampment were in the process of preparing food and packaging it. Things were being put into baskets. The children had been taken somewhere else, hopefully someplace safer. It was obvious they were preparing to leave the cave. *How are they going to get out of here? Charlie knows where they're at. He's got to have them surrounded. Assuming they manage to escape, where the hell can they go?* It hadn't occurred to Will until now, he might be the main reason why Charlie was focused on attacking these people.

Chapter 7

Even before Will and Leslie had graduated from college, he'd received notice he was about to be drafted. The two of them discussed it. Leslie wanted them to leave for Canada the day after graduation. She was adamantly against the war. He was, too, but not as passionately. His father had managed to evade being drafted during World War II. He and his father had been estranged from one another for the past several years. There was no question in anyone's mind that Will's lack of respect for his father influenced a good many of his decisions. He would ask himself, 'What would old Teddy do', then he'd do the opposite. Will's admiration and respect for Augie Nelson, and Thomas Strong also influenced his decision. They were more than mentors to him, they were heroes, men he looked up to and wanted to emulate. The only decision he had to make was, which branch of the service he'd enter. He decided on the Army, and he signed up to become a ranger. Because he was a college graduate, he was eligible to attend Officer Candidate School after completing ranger training. In an effort to placate Leslie he said, 'who knows, the stupid war may be over before I finish OCS'.

Will and Leslie had gone together through high school and they'd lived and worked together through college. They decided to elope on Christmas Eve day their senior year. They'd gone from being close friends in junior high to becoming committed partners. Their love for one another had grown stronger over the years. With graduation in sight, they decided not to put it off any longer. It would be their Christmas present to one another.

They were married by a circuit court judge at ten o'clock the snowy morning of Christmas Eve day in 1965. Their very best friends, Frank "Feisty" Noonan, and his fiancé, Sunny Strong, served as witnesses. After the brief ceremony, the two couples left the Courthouse and drove to Augie and Jeanne Nelson's resort in northern Wisconsin. All of them, except Sunny, had worked at the resort every summer for the past several years. Will regarded Augie and Jeanne as his adopted parents.

During their Christmas vacations, Will, and sometimes Leslie, would get up before dawn to accompany Thomas in 'running' his trap lines. Thomas had been trapping almost every winter since his youth. Will loved being in the company of this taciturn Indian man, and being outside in the exquisite beauty of the snow-blanketed forests. He always learned something new each time they went out together. Leslie shared the same feelings, but if the weather was nasty, she'd choose to spend time with Mary. The two of them had become like mother and daughter. Mary was sure her biological daughter, Bernadette, who had died a few years earlier, had chosen Leslie as her replacement.

It had been the plan all along for Will and Leslie to move north after college. Will was hoping to find a job teaching school. Leslie was leaning toward possibly going into social work. There was no question for either of them where they wanted to live. It was decided even before Will left for basic training that Leslie would go north and stay in 'their cabin' near the resort while he was away.

After completing basic training, they had two weeks together at the resort before he had to report for Ranger training. He went directly from there to OCS. He left for Vietnam in late January of 1967 where he joined his unit as part of the 7th Calvary Division. His first assignment was in the Central Highlands as a platoon leader. They operated out of a remote base camp sending out patrols to the surrounding small villages in search of Vietcong, weapons caches and jungle supply routes.

Before long Will began developing a respect and kind of admiration for the enemy. He was intrigued with their ingenuity and resourcefulness. What they lacked in firepower they made up for by their cunning use of the jungle as a resource, and often as a weapon. A large majority of the men under his command only wanted one thing; to put in their 365 days, and get the hell out of this miserable, godforsaken place, hopefully alive and in one piece. Lieutenants were probably the most unpopular people in Vietnam. They were the messengers who were charged with delivering orders and making sure they were executed. A lieutenant had a life expectancy of two weeks. If the VC didn't get him, one of his own would, especially if he was one of the zealous, ninety-day wonders right out of OCS, bucking for a promotion.

The primary reason Lieutenant Morrissey survived was he took care of his men. If he received orders that involved unnecessary risk and he thought they were absurdly impossible, he'd sit down with his sergeants to figure out some way of revising the plan to increase the odds of survival. They had a job to do. He saw his job as doing what could be done from a practical standpoint, but his personal mission was to get his men through their year long tour of duty alive, and, if possible, unscathed.

When Will learned the rangers were starting up a tactically elite force of small reconnaissance units he jumped at the chance. A part of his reasoning was that reconnaissance was about collecting accurate information about the enemy. It was a challenge that attracted most of the men who signed up to become LRRPs.

Daredevils were weeded out. They could put a mission in jeopardy. Will saw it as a way to possibly enhance 'military intelligence', an oxymoron in his opinion. If anyone paid attention to the information they gathered it might help to keep men alive and lead to a quicker end to this insane war.

Chapter 8

It was clear, a decision had been made by Phong Dieu and his lieutenants to evacuate the caves. The Vietcong knew their location. They had an incentive to avenge the casualties they'd suffered. Maybe they also knew these people had found and rescued the 'Yankee prisoner'. Will sensed it wouldn't be long before they'd launch a major attack to dislodge them from the mountain, and kill as many of them as possible. They'd been probing for weaknesses up until now. Will observed several days had gone by with no outside visitors showing up bringing in supplies. He was certain the VC had them blockaded and under siege. They'd been doing what they did best...wear their foe down by attrition and patiently waiting for the right moment to strike. It looked like that moment was imminent. He tried to communicate a strategy of defense with drawings. Phong Dieu studied Will's crude sketches. He indicated he understood and he made adjustments in the way he deployed his small force of men. Will knew that one of two things needed to happen. Neither of them seemed likely. They either needed the cavalry to come riding in with strong reinforcements, or they needed to figure out a means of escaping. He wondered if there was a back door exit to the caves. If there was, did Charlie know about it?

Will considered his own options. He knew he was a liability. His upper body was nearly healed, but with his infected leg he wouldn't be able to travel any distance under his own steam. He doubted these people would abandon him. Will settled on a plan that would free them from the burden of caring for him and at the same time deal a blow to the enemy. He remembered the cache of weapons Phong Dieu had shown him. He would make himself into a bomb and sneak into the VC encampment.

He knew time was running out and he had to act soon, perhaps tonight. He wanted to find a way to write a letter to Leslie explaining what had happened with the hope that it might somehow get to her. It was like a note in a bottle written by a desperate castaway. The problem was he hadn't seen anything that even resembled paper or a pencil. He wondered whether these people even had a written language. After searching for something he could write on, an idea came to him. He located the rifle crates and was able to remove one of the boards from one of the crate tops. He confiscated a knife that was used for meal preparation. He set about carving a terse message he'd given considerable thought to. He used a bullet tip to write out the letters on the board. 'Les, love u. Died 4 others. Find love, W." He painfully began to inscribe the message. Phong Dieu noticed what he was doing, and he watched for a while.

Will didn't concern himself with anyone knowing what he was saying. The challenge was to get these people to carry the message with them. The odds were, Leslie would never see it.

It had become common-place to hear drum messages throughout the day, and even into the night. The drum began sounding as Will worked at carving his message. He listened and watched to see if it provoked a sense of urgency, or alarm. Everyone responded to this message by stopping what they were doing. When the drumming stopped there was a great deal of chatter. Will set the board aside and picked up his crutch, along with his rifle and ammo bag. He made his way to where Phong Dieu and several other men were standing just outside of the cave entrance. They all seemed to be facing one of the trails that led up the mountain.

After several minutes three soldiers dressed in camo fatigues appeared climbing up the trail. As they neared the ledge, Will could see two of the men were Americans, the third looked Laotian and he greeted Phong Dieu. He politely introduced the Americans. Will hobbled toward them. One of them, a tall well built black man, saw him and asked, if he was Lieutenant Willis Morrissey. He nodded. The soldier smiled broadly and extended his hand to him, "I'm Lieutenant McMurray, Clayton McMurray, this is Sergeant Matt Cooper, and this is Corporal Bahk Thieu. Bahk is our Hmong interpreter." Will shook hands with all three. "We've been looking for you since Christmas eve, Lieutenant. We're here to take you home." Will still said nothing. McMurray's smile faded. "Lieutenant, are you okay? Can you hear me?"

Will couldn't hold back his tears, "Yes, I just can't believe you're here. I can't believe you found me." He wiped his tears. "I never thought," Will stopped. "I gave up hoping... it's been so long. I don't..."

The big Lieutenant gave Will a fatherly hug and tugged on Will's long sandy beard. "Nice disguise."

Will stepped back and pointed to his leg. Lieutenant McMurray stooped down to look at it, with the bone still protruding. "Sweet Jesus, have you had this all along?" He nodded. "Can you walk on it at all?"

"A little, but not far, and not fast."

"This is going to call for a change in plans." McMurray stood and looked at Will. "Did this happen when you fell from the chopper?" Will nodded, wondering what 'a change in plans' meant. McMurray consulted with his Sgt. Cooper and Cooper took off down the trail.

McMurray turned back to Will. "Don't worry. We're

going ahead with the extraction. It's just that we thought you'd be more mobile. We'd planned to escort you to a safe place for a dust-off. We wanted to try to avoid letting Charlie know where these people are."

Will interrupted him, "Clayton, Charlie already knows they're here. These people have to get out of here like yesterday. I think Charlie is about to launch a big attack. We need help. We're low on ammo. We need reinforcements. We need air support. What we really need is a major dust-off operation to air-lift all of us out of here. I don't think we stand a chance down below. I'm surprised you were able to get in here. I'm pretty sure Charlie has this place surrounded"

"I hear you. First off, let me correct you. As of now, it is us and them. You keep using the word 'we'. You're no longer a part of the scene here. Secondly, we haven't got very much to say about anything that happens with these people, or about anything that happens here. We're in Laos, not Vietnam. We're not supposed to be here. My orders are to extract you and try to get all of us back safe and sound." McMurray softened his tone. "Look Will, I'm sorry as hell. There's nothing I'd like more than to try to help these people, but I have very specific orders."

"Who are you guys anyway? What are you?"

"We're Navy SEALs. We're trained to do special operations, weird shit like this." McMurray asked if Phong Dieu was the head honcho. Will nodded. He turned to his interpreter, "Bahk, explain to this man we're taking Lieutenant Morrissey with us. Tell him we understand that the Vietcong are on to his location and that he needs to get out of here as well. Ask him if he has any way to safely evacuate his people from here."

The interpreter Bahk spoke back and fourth with Phong Dieu. Several times during their discussion, Phong Dieu gestured toward the cave. Bahk then reported the conversation to McMurray. "Phong Dieu understands the situation with the Vietcong. He's been trying to hold out hoping help would arrive. He knows we can't help him to evacuate all of his people. They've been determined not to abandon the Lieutenant. He says they do have a plan for evacuation." Bahk pointed to the cave. "Phong Dieu says the cave grows narrow, and splits into two passages. One passage goes up and comes out further up the mountain on the other side. The other goes down and comes out on the other side close to the jungles. Both passages are only wide enough for one person to crawl through at-a-time. He says it wouldn't be possible for Lieutenant Morrissey to squeeze his way through parts of the cave because of his leg. It's difficult even for small people."

"Ask Phong Dieu, how soon he and his people can be ready to evacuate. Ask him how much time it will take for them to get through the caves. Most importantly, will they be safe when they get to the jungles on the other side."

Bahk and Phong Dieu conversed again. Bahk reported, "Phong Dieu says that they've already begun moving the women, children and elders. He will maintain a rear guard to make sure the Vietcong don't overtake the others. He has no idea of how safe they'll be on the other side. He can only hope that the Vietcong are concentrating their assault on this location. He doesn't know if they're aware of the passages."

McMurray told Bahk to tell Phong Dieu, "I am going to ask for some help. I'm going to request an air strike of fighter planes that will drop napalm on the jungles below. That ought to give them time to make their escape. Phong Dieu had no idea what Napalm was. Bahk explained they were fire bombs that would burn the jungle below and everything in the forest.

Phong Dieu looked pleased. He told Bahk he'd like

to stay to watch the napalm."

McMurray told Bahk to tell Phong Dieu he was welcome to do so, but when the bombing was over, Charlie wasn't going to be very happy and they'll probably be looking to kick some major ass." Will said to Clayton, "I'd sure like to hear how that comes out in translation."

Clayton smiled his broad grin. "I'm surprised you haven't learned to speak at least some of their language, Will. Christ you've been missing close to five months. How long were you captive before these guys got to you?"

"I have no idea. I was unconscious for days, maybe two or three weeks. I don't know. Charlie abandoned me in the jungles. It was a few days after I regained consciousness that these people came along. They literally carried me out of the jungles and brought me up here. That took a few days" Will looked at Phong Dieu. "These people have been very kind to me, Clayton. I owe them." I'm glad you're able to help them."

"I hope it helps, Will. I hope Charlie's not waiting for them on the other side. It's going to help us, too. I didn't know you were this busted up and wouldn't be able to walk out of here. I'm calling for a dust off from right here. If all goes well, the choppers will arrive about the time the bombing begins. The original plan was to slip in, grab you and slip out. We didn't want to tip Charlie off about where these Hmong fighters were holed-up." Will asked what he called them. "Hmong," he spelled the word for him. "The Hmong are tribal groups of people. They live separate from the Laotians. They're kind of like the bushmen in Africa, or the aborigines in Australia. Actually they're scattered all over most of Asia, even China. They live according to very strict traditions and are ancestor worshipers. They reject a good part of the changes of the modern world. They more or less live off the land. They'd be perfectly content if they could have their own chunk of the planet, and the rest of the world would just leave them alone." Clayton went to the edge of the precipice in front of the cave. Will followed. "The irony is these are, as you say, a very gentle people, but they've proven to be real kick-ass fighters when it comes to the VC." Will could vouch for that.

Clayton surveyed the ledge. "We haven't got enough landing area to set a chopper down here. We've got two of them. One to provide machine gun support. The two of us will be lifted into the first one. We can probably airlift their guns and ammo out of here and haul it over the mountain for them. That will help speed up their escape. We don't want it falling into Charlie's hands. I'll see if we can get them a few cases of M-16's, ammo and grenades. We might even be able to get them a few mortars." He turned to Will. "Is that going to make you feel any better?"

"Some."

"I Gotta tell you, Will, they showed us pictures of you that were taken back when they first found you. You looked like hell. I sure wouldn't have recognized you from them. Man, with your long hair and beard, you look like one of those hippie, war-protestor types back home."

"I gotta tell you Clayton, this war sucks shit. I might just join them."

"Just between you and me, I am inclined to agree. Charlie's one tenacious little mother. Short of nuking this whole country, I think Charlie will prevail in the end. This is nothing but a waste of lives and tax-payer money. The only ones benefiting from it are some corporations and a bunch of politicians, but you never heard me say that."

Two more team members seemed to materialize on the ledge. One of them carried radio equipment.

Clayton introduced them to Will. The radioman put him in contact with one of Clayton's superiors. Clayton explained the situation and asked for an air strike. Using a detailed topographical map he choreographed the helicopter extraction. He gave out times and coordinates for the air strike. None of his requests were challenged. The person he was talking to gave him a precise time the planes would arrive and commence their attack. He turned to Phong Dieu and had Bahk explain the plan to him. He seemed especially pleased they wouldn't have to take their cache of weapons with them. Within fifteen minutes all of the Hmong people were gone except for Phong Dieu and his small band of rear guard.

Will had to get off his feet. He sat down on a boulder near the cave entrance. *I'd give just about anything for another one of the leaves the medicine man was giving me.* Everyone else was busy doing something. He felt utterly exhausted. *Five months. It's been five freaking months.* He thought about Leslie. As time had gone by he'd begun to wonder if she'd stopped waiting, thinking he was dead. He longed to hold her again, but he also felt a sense of fear. *What if she gave up hope? What if she's found someone else? What if something's happened to her?* How was all of this going to affect the two of them? He knew that things would never be the same for him, but what about them, what about their relationship'? He stopped himself from ruminating and tried to bring his attention back to the present. He found himself reminiscing about these past few months, and all he'd been through with these people. Clayton's earlier question, 'how come you didn't learn to speak their language', bothered him. He'd picked up a few words, mostly the names of objects, or body parts. No words pertaining to feelings or ideas. To some extent they'd learned to communicate in non-verbal ways. He felt a deep respect for these people. He was beginning to realize having been with them had affected him in ways he'd never forget.

Will looked at Phong Dieu. He wondered if he'd ever see this man again. They'd saved one another's lives more than once. Will felt he'd never be able to balance the scale. It had been just a few hours ago he'd come to realize the sacrifice Phong Dieu and his people were about to make to try to save him. That's when he'd decided on a plan to end his own life, to free them from the burden of caring for him. Charlie was in for a big surprise. He was about to experience a fire-breathing dragon. If Charlie survived the inferno he was going to discover the Hmong had vanished. Will wondered about the other Hmong groups in the area. Were they going be in jeopardy, too?

Suddenly everyone's attention went skyward. They could hear the thumping sound of the choppers before they could see them. Then they heard the growling, hissing sound of the fighter jets. There were six of them and they came in low dropping the napalm bombs in rows moving from the center out to either side. Everyone watched their first pass. Clayton waved for Phong Dieu and his men to go. The first helicopter came into position and dropped a line with a harness. Will and Bahk were lifted into the chopper. It moved to take a defensive position allowing the other one to take it's place. The crates of weapons and ammo had been lashed together into three stacks. After they were lifted into the chopper it labored to gain altitude with the weight of the load.

Once Clayton and Cooper were safely aboard the first chopper the pilots headed for a location Phong Dieu had pointed out on a map. Will and Clayton assumed that's where Phong Dieu intended to go next, unless Charlie was lying in wait and came at them. Then all bets were off. They probably wouldn't survive.

Clayton scanned the jungles below through binoculars hoping not to spot any VC. "Christ, what a beautiful place. Who'd ever guess it's such a dangerous piece of real estate?"

Chapter 9

It was a sunny but cool late April morning. Leslie left the cabin and went to the heavy wire cage Thomas had built for Merlin to protect and confine him. After she removed his hood Merlin cautiously stepped onto the gauntlet making a short soft murmuring sound. She took him to the upright log that sat in the front yard. She talked to him complimenting him on what a handsome fellow he was. After the hawk stepped onto the log she tethered him and put a raw chicken leg on the log. She watched him for a few moments before returning to the cabin to gather the things she'd need for the day.

When she came back out she had a backpack slung over her shoulder and a cup of coffee. The gauntlet was tucked under her arm. All of her clothes hung on her as she'd lost more than twenty pounds since Christmas. She was preoccupied as she strode toward the log to retrieve Merlin. Mary had been telling her Will was getting stronger. Leslie hoped Will would someday be able to see Merlin. She looked up as she neared the log and felt a jolt of panic. Merlin wasn't on the log. She scanned the yard. The hawk wasn't anywhere to be seen. She stood frozen by fear. She looked toward the trees that surrounded the cabin on three sides. This far north spring was slow in coming. It would be a month before the leaves achieved full maturity. She was almost at the stage of full panic, when she heard a screech. She looked up. "Oh my God," Leslie put her hand to her mouth. There was Merlin circling above. He screeched again as if to say, "Hey, Leslie, look! No hands." He was about thirty feet off the ground. He glided toward the lake, caught a slight updraft, circled back and swooped down toward the log perch. He was unable to control his descent perfectly, his talons grazed the log and he landed awkwardly a few feet beyond. By the time Leslie reached him he had his primary feathers crossed behind him. She almost laughed out loud. "Merlin, if birds could show embarrassment, your face would be crimson right now." She put the glove on and stooped. Merlin stepped up onto her arm, and she placed him on the log. She stroked his head while telling him how proud she was of him, and how beautiful he looked gliding. "Landings are a bitch, Merlin." She attributed Merlin's awkward landing to the lack of strength in his shoulder, and leg. "That will come. The important thing is that you're finally able to fly."

She went back to the cabin and called Thomas and Mary. Thomas answered the phone, sounding cheerful. "Here Leslie, I think you need to talk to Mary." When Mary's voice came on the line she sounded even more cheerful. "You've received a sign from the hawk."

"Merlin took off on his own and he flew briefly."

"Will's been found, Leslie. I thought he was a goner yesterday, but he's alive. He's safe now." Mary laughed joyfully, "Call Augie and Jeanne. I'll hang up. We can talk later."

Leslie got Merlin on the gauntlet, carried him to the jeep and put him in the cage. Their one-eyed golden lab, Gabe, jumped up and got on the seat next to her. She drove to the resort and bounded up the stairs not bothering to knock as she entered the house. Augie was in the midst of making breakfast. "Augie, Will's been found. He's alive. Mary says he's safe."

"Did the Army call you?"

"No, but Merlin took off this morning and flew. I called Mary and she told me the good news about Will."

Augie knew he shouldn't doubt Mary, or the significance of the hawk flying, especially since the two messages coincided. "But, we don't know for sure."

"Augie," Leslie pleaded. "How much more sure can we be?"

Jeanne entered the kitchen. She'd caught the conversation on her way to the kitchen. "I agree, Mary wouldn't tell Leslie Will was safe it if she wasn't sure of it." She and Leslie hugged one another.

Leslie called Feisty and Sunny, but no one answered. "Damn, they must have already left for the day." She called Sunny's work number. She'd just arrived and was excited with the news. She knew Feisty was out in the field today inspecting a project. She'd try to get hold of him. Leslie decided it would be best not to call Will's mother until they'd received official word. She called Norma to share the news. Leslie was working with Norma four or five days a week. Norma was thrilled for her. She told Leslie to not come in today, she could manage by herself.

Leslie had no sooner hung up with Norma when the phone rang again. Leslie answered expecting to hear Feisty at the other end. She was surprised to hear Will's mother's voice at the other end. Helen said, "I tried calling your place, Leslie. I figured you might be at the resort." Helen hesitated briefly, "I don't want to burden you, but I thought you should know. I just learned that Will's father died last night. He apparently had a massive heart attack. He was dead by the time the ambulance arrived. I don't know if you knew, but Ted moved out in February and was living with a lady friend of his. She called this morning to tell me."

"I'm sorry Helen. No, I didn't know you were separated." Leslie decided not to say anything to her about Will being rescued until they'd received official word. There was the remote possibility it wasn't true.

Leslie asked if Helen and Jerome were going to be okay with Ted gone. Helen told her she'd gotten Ted to take out a life insurance policy last year. They'd be okay for the time being. Jerome was talking about enlisting in the Marines after he graduated in June. She was opposed to his decision, but if he did, she was going to sell the house and find herself a small apartment.

After hanging up, Leslie told Augie and Jeanne about Will's father dying last night. Augie said, "I can't say I'm filled with remorse. It's just too bad he wasn't able to learn his son is alive and has been rescued." Augie hesitated, "I guess if he'd lived for another 50 years things wouldn't have ever changed between them. Will couldn't do anything right as far a he was concerned. I wonder how Helen's going to manage financially."

They talked briefly about Helen. Augie was skeptical that Ted would have taken out a very large policy on himself. "The premiums on a big dollar policy for a man his age would be over a thousand dollars a year. Ted was too cheap and too petty to provide Helen with that kind of security."

Leslie had breakfast with them. She decided to go to Norma's anyway. "I'll go crazy if I just sit around here. You know how the Army is about letting people know anything. Will might get here before they show up to tell us he's okay." She left Gabe with them. It was a twenty-five mile drive from the resort to Norma's place.

Everyone was surprised when a telegram arrived early that afternoon from the Department of Defense informing Leslie that her husband, Lieutenant Willis Morrissey, had been found alive, and had been rescued. He was being transferred to an Army hospital in the Philippines. More information would be forthcoming as it became available. Jeanne called Leslie at Norma's to give her the 'official word'. Leslie was concerned about the need for Will to require hospitalization. 'Was it a matter of routine procedure, or was Will in bad shape'? She asked if Jeanne would please call Will's mother with the news. "I'll be home in a while."

Norma and Leslie celebrated with a beer. Norma revealed she'd had a real problem with alcohol a few years back. "I like beer. I like it a lot. I limit myself to one a day. If I'm upset about something and don't think I can stop at just one, I don't let myself have any. Before leaving for home, Norma cautioned Leslie not to let Merlin overdo the flying. She warned he could end up re-injuring himself by stressing the weak muscles and tendons or by crash landing. She emphasized that Leslie double check his tether. "It was either too loose, or he's smarter than the average hawk. Withhold feeding him before letting him fly so you can entice him back with food when you feel he's flown enough." Leslie wanted to know how she could tell how much exercise was enough. "Just do it gradually, letting him have a little more time each day. When he makes an awkward landing, or you see him favoring the wing or the leg, rein him in. Maybe even back off for a day or two."

Leslie spent the evening with Augie and Jeanne. It was too cold to sit outside for a sunset. They sat inside before the fireplace, Augie with his martini, and the ladies with their wine. Feisty called. Augie and he conversed at some length before Leslie and he talked. Feisty wondered, "How come he's in need of medical attention? Damn it, they shouldn't tell you anything if they're not going to tell you the complete story. I mean, Christ, now we have to sit here and worry about how serious it is." He apologized for sounding so critical.

"No, you're right Feisty. You'd think by now they would have learned how to handle loved ones with more sensitivity. I just wish I could talk to him, I want to hear his voice."

At two o'clock the next morning the phone rang at

the cabin. Leslie was awakened from a sound sleep, "Les?" The voice at the other end sounded gravelly and tentative. She was struggling to awaken herself fully. "It's me. Will."

"Oh, my God, Will, it's you." She was instantly awake. "Where are you? How are you? Are you okay?"

"I'm okay, Les. God, it's good to hear your voice." She was crying almost convulsively as she struggled to pull on a robe. She could hear Gabe's tail thumping. He slept at the foot of their bed. The cabin was cold. He followed her as she went to turn up the thermostat. "Where are you? When can I see you?"

"I'm at an Army hospital. I'm in the Philippines. They brought me here today. I don't know how long I'll be here." He asked, "Les, are you okay?"

"I'm fine, Will. We're all fine." She stretched the telephone cord to grab a counter stool and put it in front of the space heater. She was beginning to shiver. She gave a nervous laugh. "Thomas called me this morning." She looked at the clock. "I mean yesterday morning. Mary told me you'd been rescued." She started crying some more. "Oh, Will, this is too good to be true."

"I know, Les. There have been moments when I thought I'd never see you again."

"Can you talk, Will? Can you tell me what's wrong?"

"Yeah, I'm alone right now." He asked, "What time is it there?" She told him. "I'm sorry. It's about eight o'clock in the morning here, the next day. I didn't know how to calculate what time it would be there."

"Will, don't apologize. I'm just glad to hear your voice."

He was having to make an effort to speak. "Les, my right leg got busted up pretty badly the day I was captured. It's below the knee. It never got fixed in all this time. The leg's infected. I don't know if they're going to be able to save it. It looks like my days of ass-kicking contests are about over."

"Will, I want to be there with you. I want to be there for you."

"Hang in there, Les. I think they plan to fly me to Hawaii in a couple of days. I'll let you know what's happening." They talked for a few more minutes, before someone came into Will's room to wheel him elsewhere for more testing. After hanging up it occurred to her she hadn't mentioned Merlin. It was a story that needed time to be told. It could wait.

Leslie was too wide-awake to bother going back to bed. She started coffee, took a hot shower, and dressed in layers again. The day dawned overcast and a few flakes of snow were meandering to the ground. After feeding Gabe she went outside and removed Merlin from his cage. She put him on the log/perch but he made no effort to fly. She decided it was probably because there weren't updraft air currents with weather like this. She tethered him before offering him some food. Gabe kept his distance from the hawk, not out of fear on his part, but out of obedience. Leslie was more concerned about preventing stress to Merlin. Will had spent a lot of time working with the dog and Gabe did what he was told. In a way he provided her with another emotional link to Will. Gabe was a gentle soul who sensed her needs. He was there for her when she needed him, and he demanded very little. She often found herself 'thinking out loud' to him, something she'd come to do a lot.

Leslie stopped at the resort to tell Jeanne and Augie about her brief conversation with Will. Augie asked if she wanted him to make travel arrangements for her to go to the Philippines. She declined saying Will might end up being transferred before she could even get there.

On the way to Norma's, Leslie thought about the

parallels between Will's and Merlin's injuries. They'd both had their legs broken. Was it the same leg for both of them? She wondered if Will had sustained other injuries besides the leg. Had his shoulder been injured, too? Mary said that it was. Was it the same one as Merlin's? To top it all off, it had happened to both of them on the same date. It seemed incomprehensible that such similar things had happened to a man and a beast who were half-a-world apart and Mary had envisioned both events.

Chapter 10

The two helicopters set down at the Da Nang air base close to mid-night. An ambulance was waiting to take Will to the base hospital. Clayton told him he was to be taken to a medical/surgical unit first, then probably on to the Philippines. "I'll stop by to see you before you leave here. We've got a debriefing." They shook hands rather than salute.

"Thanks Clayton. Thanks for everything. I appreciate what you did to help those people."

"Let's hope Charlie wasn't waiting for them and they were able to make a clean getaway. The CIA is working closely with the Hmong. They supply them with weapons and they do a lot of intelligence gathering by monitoring the Hmong communication network. It was through them we learned that some Hmong had found and rescued you and where they'd taken you. The CIA's been pretty cooperative with us. I'll see what I can find out about the folks you were with."

Upon arrival at the base hospital, Will was immediately taken into an emergency room. Two doctors examined him. Blood samples were drawn and he underwent a series of x-rays. An orthopedic surgeon examined him and an IV drip of strong antibiotics was started. In Will's opinion he thought the infection in his leg was starting to flare up again. It had looked better a couple of days ago.

It was late afternoon before he was finally admitted to a room by himself. He was exhausted. As soon as he laid down he felt dizzy and nauseated. He threw back the sheets, and grabbed a waste basket. He hadn't eaten anything since the night before. Nothing came up. When the nausea subsided, he sat on the edge of the bed. There was a knock on the door, and an officer entered. He quickly appraised the situation, seeing Will holding the waste basket between his legs."

He started to turn to seek a nurse. Will stopped him." I'm okay, Sir. I just need to get out of this fucking air-conditioning. It's making me sick." The officer was a Colonel. It turned out that he was also a psychiatrist. He immediately went and turned off the room's air conditioning unit, opened a window and closed the door. In a few minutes the room's temperature and humidity level began to rise.

The Colonel introduced himself. "I'm Dave Bowen." They shook hands. "Are you up to talking, Will? May I call you Will?" He nodded. "I won't stick around very long." Colonel Bowen stood next to the bed. "You've really been through a lot these past few months, Will. I dropped by to see how you're doing." He paused. "Will, people who've been through the kind of things you've been through often find themselves feeling kind of panicky once they're no longer in danger. It's like it kind of catches up with them all at once." He waited to see if Will had anything to say. "I know you're not ready to talk about what you've been through. I just want you to know, if you find yourself ready to hit the panic button, please let somebody know. It's more the rule, than the exception. You're not crazy. What's crazy is what you've been through. We're all here for you." Bowen studied Will. "See, I told you I wasn't going to stick around long."

Will looked at Bowen. "Thanks Colonel, thanks for getting rid of the air-conditioning."

"Do you need anything else?"

"Yeah, but I don't know if you can help me. I need a gun." Will paused. "Don't worry, Doc. I'm not going to go wacko and shoot up the place, and I'm not going to grease myself. I just need one."

"I don't know," Bowen said. "Would a pistol do?"

"I don't care. I just need something."

"Let me see what I can do. I doubt 'the powers that be' will be keen on the idea. Never mind that they all sleep with loaded weapons nearby. All I can do is try." Will thanked him and Bowen left.

Will dozed fitfully for a couple of hours. He was awakened once by a nurse who came in to take his vitals. The nurse startled Will, and apologized for waking him. It was early morning and still dark when Clayton McMurray knocked and came into the dimly lit room. "Hey, I see you got the air-conditioning turned off. Good for you. I hate the damn things" McMurray approached the bed. "How you doing, Will?"

Will shrugged." I had a conversation with an Army shrink named Bowen a little while ago."

"Yeah, I know." Clayton reached into a bag. "Bowen asked me to give you this." He produced a semi-automatic pistol. "It's loaded with blanks. Sorry, regulations don't allow live ammo. Actually, regs don't allow for patients to have any kind of weapon. Not even a squirt gun."

Will smiled. "Thanks Clayton. I really appreciate this."

"Now don't go waving this thing around or they'll relieve you of it poste haste." Clayton laughed as he pulled up a chair." Bowen wrote a fuckin' prescription for it. Pharmacy gave birth to a brick. They didn't know what to do. I'm just kidding. He went straight to the base commander to get permission."

Clayton and Will visited for close to an hour. He reported the Hmong people who Will had been with were able to escape the mountain safely. "Apparently Charlie wasn't aware of the back door exit. The napalm attack wouldn't have been nearly as effective if it had been a month earlier. The jungle had time to dry out after the rainy season ended. It created an inferno." Some of their conversation centered around their personal lives. Little mention was made of the rescue operation that had brought them together. Clayton asked Will how much he remembered about the 'dust-off' operation the day he went missing. Will recounted the situation and the conditions up to the point he lost consciousness after falling from the chopper.

"I read through the debriefings given by the chopper crews and the five men you were with that day. Their reports are pretty consistent. The pilot of the chopper you tried to board has refused to fly since. He blames himself for losing you. He's convinced if he hadn't panicked and he'd hung in there for another ten seconds you'd have been home free." Will asked if any of the others felt that way, were they down on him. "They all said you'd managed to make it to the chopper when he started to lift off. They blame themselves for not reacting fast enough to get hold of you. The pilot made a judgment call. He was afraid if he dropped back down to get you, he'd be running the risk of losing everyone. He said you were under intense fire from a force of about forty VC, plus the weather conditions were deteriorating by the second."

"He's right. If I'd been in his shoes I'd have done the same thing. We were all amazed the choppers even showed up, given the weather conditions. I'm surprised any of us were able to make it to the choppers alive. I'm sure the downpour was affecting the velocity and range of the bullets that were flying from both sides." Clayton asked if Will had been subjected to torture. "As far as I know I was unconscious for weeks. If I did regain consciousness during that period of time I've blocked it out." He told Clayton about the condition he was in when he became consciously aware that he'd been taken captive. Clayton told Will his team had been shown pictures the Hmong took of him and the VC encampment right after they'd found him. When Clayton arose to leave, Will said to him, "They're probably going to transfer me out of here tomorrow. Next stop the Philippines."

"I'm glad we found you, Will. It's going to take you a while to pull yourself back together. Don't expect yourself to be the same person you were, and don't expect the people around you to be the same either. It's not a matter of catching up. It's almost a matter of meeting up with long lost friends and seeing if you still have anything going with one another."

Will was awakened at regular intervals to have his vitals taken and more blood drawn. He had to insist the staff leave the air conditioning off. Right after breakfast a barber came in to shave his beard and cut his tangled mop of hair. Afterward he held a mirror for Will to see himself. He was almost alarmed at how sunken his cheeks were. As the barber was about to leave another person came in and began giving Will a manicure and pedicure. Will objected but was told that this was according to orders. In the process of administering the pedicure the technician looked at his leg. "Holy shit, what happened to you?" He pointed to the protruding bone. "That looks like it hurts. Does it?"

"Only when I get it caught in a ladder rung."

"Sorry Lieutenant. It's just that I've never seen a broken leg like that before." The technician said, "It looks like it's been that way for a while. When did it happen?"

"Christmas Eve day,"

"Holy shit, and nothing was done about it before now?"

"I was captured by the VC on 12/24."

"Holy shit, you've been a POW all this time? How

the hell did you escape with your leg like this?"

"It's a long story."

"Sorry Lieutenant, you probably don't want to talk about it." The manicurist refrained from asking any further questions. Will closed his eyes. He found himself thinking about Phong Dieu, the medicine man, the woman he'd stood guard with and several of the others he'd spent time with. He began to feel a sense of remorse. *It wasn't until the last day or two I realized they were sticking around because they couldn't take me with them. Otherwise they would have left earlier before things got so bad.* He recalled his decision to end his life just before Clayton and his crew showed up. He thought to himself he should be feeling grateful that all of them had managed to make it out of there alive. *So why am I feeling so Goddamned depressed?* He thought about asking to see Colonel Bowen. He thought, *I should be happy as hell to be out of there and to be safe. Look at me, I'm fucking miserable.*

There was a light knock on the door, and Colonel Bowen entered the room tentatively. "Ah you're awake." As Bowen approached the bed he could see streaks of tears on Will's cheeks. "You look really different without the beard and the long hair." He studied Will. "Not that you don't look dashing this way, but I kind of liked the other look better. It was less military."

Will's retort was. "I look like a fucking concentration camp survivor."

"It's coming down on you hard, isn't it?" Will didn't respond. Bowen pulled up a chair and sat. "Will, what you're going through is typical. You're depressed as hell. Talking about it isn't going to help right now. It may even make things worse. A lot of times people who've been through a prolonged ordeal start self- medicating themselves. They turn to alcohol, or dope. A lot of them become addicted to speed."

Will asked sarcastically," So what do you recommend?"

"I recommend staying alive and meeting this thing bits at a time. If you try to take all of it on at one time, it's going to defeat you."

"What's 'this fucking thing', Doc?" Bowen threw it back at him asking what Will thought 'it' was. Will shook his head.

Bowen waited before asking, "What's scaring you, Will?" After several moments Bowen pursed his lips, as if deciding whether to say anything more. "Will, let me throw an idea out to you. You don't have to respond right this minute. I'd just like for you to give it some thought." Will waited. "Okay, so here's the idea. It's not complicated. It's simply this. Sometimes when we're running toward something, we're also trying to run away from something else. We're trying to escape from that thing we're afraid of. We're thinking, if we can manage to get a to a place we think is safe, we'll be okay, all will be well." Bowen shrugged, "That's it."

The two of them sat in silence for a while. Will finally spoke. "Are you saying I think if I can just make it home everything's going to be okay, the past will just go away?"

"What do you think?"

"I don't know. I'm afraid of what the people back home are going to feel when they see what's happened to me. I mean, I'm a mess. I feel like fucking Humpty Dumpty. I've fallen off the wall, and no one's ever going to be able to put me back together again."

"You're right, Will. You're a mess. You're also right about another thing. No one's going to be able to put you back together again. You're going to have to do most of it yourself. Furthermore, you'll never be the same person. There are a couple of words I like. One's 'grit' the other one is 'gumption'. They kind of go hand in hand, 'guts, ' and 'determination'. You've got both.

Otherwise you wouldn't be here now. You'd have died out there in the jungles months ago." Will ran a hand over his short cropped hair and touched his face expecting to feel his beard. Bowen cleared his throat, "Will, maybe I'm pressing my luck, and pushing you too hard. I'm not sure I should even bring this up." He decided to forge ahead. "I know you've had some moments of what you regard as weakness, moments when you didn't think you could go on." He paused. "No one who's gone through an ordeal like what you've been through, escapes feeling that way."

Will couldn't look at Bowen. "Yeah, I had moments like that. I had lots of them before the Hmong people rescued me. I probably would have done it, if I'd had the means."

Bowen asked gently, "What about after you were rescued by them."

Will glanced at him, and in almost a whisper he said. "Yeah, I decided I had to end things." He was trying to fight back tears. "Doc, the place was surrounded by VC. I knew those people weren't going to abandon me. I also knew they couldn't escape with me. I decided to cut them free."

Bowen, waited before asking, "When was this Will? When did you decide you needed to end your life?"

Will gave a slight sardonic laugh, "Get this Doc. Talk about irony. Right before the Seals team showed up. If they'd arrived fifteen minutes later, they'd, have brought me back in a body bag."

Bowen said, "But of course you had no way of knowing they were on their way to rescue you, did you?" Will shook his head. "So why then? Why that particular time?"

Will looked up at Bowen and held Bowen's steady gaze. "Because I was sure Charlie was about to launch an all out attack." Will wiped his cheeks. "I decided if I checked out, they'd be free to escape. Charlie knew where we were, they had the fucking mountain sealed off. Those people would have been slaughtered, every last one of them."

"That sounds like an act of bravery, not cowardice, Will. You made the decision to sacrifice your life to save the lives of your friends." Bowen touched Will's arm. "I have absolutely no doubt you would have done it."

"So," Will looked at Bowen again, "why does that make me scared of going home?"

"Well, this is just a guess on my part," Bowen said as he shifted his position on the chair. "It sounds to me like you were between a rock and a hard place. You were torn between two fiercely strong loyalties. On the one hand you felt a strong sense of obligation toward those Hmong people. On the other hand, you've struggled to survive all of this time out of a deep sense of love and longing for the folks you love back home." Bowen rubbed his neck. "It sounds to me like a hell-of-a-tough decision. Either way you chose to go, someone was going to end up suffering." He showed a slight smile. "Good thing the cavalry showed up when it did." He patted Will's leg and stood. "I try not to offer advice, Will. Most people don't follow it anyway. However, my advice to you is to let yourself off the hook. Don't waste one precious minute of your life feeling guilty about that decision. It was made under desperate circumstances. Get on with your life." They shook hands and Bowen wished Will a good life before he started for the door. He turned back. "I almost forgot, Lieutenant McMurray gave me a parcel. It's a board you were engraving when his team arrived. Do you want it?"

"Would you get rid of it for me, Doc?"

"With pleasure. That's a good first step, Will."

Chapter 11

Leslie was surprised to see Thomas at the resort when she arrived early the next day. He and Augie were sitting at the counter having coffee. "Thomas, you're here early, how come?"

"I was up all night with Mary. She's feeling poorly. I ended up taking her to the hospital around five this morning. They're running tests on her and I was kind of in the way. So I decided to come out here."

"What do they think's wrong with her?

"They think maybe it's her heart, but they don't know for sure. She started having trouble breathing yesterday. I kept insisting we go to the hospital. She finally indulged me when it started getting worse early this morning." He shook his head. "She's hated hospitals for as far back as I can remember."

Jeanne came into the kitchen. She'd gone to get dressed. She and Leslie greeted one another and she asked if there was any further word about what was happening with Will. "He called late last night. He's going to be flown to Hawaii tomorrow. He has a serious infection in his right leg. He doesn't know how long he'll be there." Augie asked how he sounded. Leslie avoided answering directly. "He says they've got him on pain meds which he's grateful for, but they make him feel like he's in a fog."

Thomas and Augie got up from the counter stools. Augie told Leslie, "We're going into town to see how Mary's doing. We've got some shopping to do and things to take care of. You're welcome to join us." Leslie was torn. She was due at Norma's and she had Merlin and Gabe with her, but she also wanted to see Mary. They worked it out so Merlin's cage would be transferred to the back of Thomas's enclosed truck. Leslie wouldn't stay long. She called Norma to let her know she'd be late.

At the hospital they were given directions to Mary's room. They stopped at the nurse's station. Thomas asked how Mary was doing and if they could see her.

"She's doing much better. Doctor Baime's her physician. He's still here. I'll let him know you're back. I know he'll want to talk with you." The nurse led them to Mary's room. "Mary, you've got guests." They were relieved to see her sitting up in bed, with her usual pleasant smile.

The doctor came to the room a few minutes later. He introduced himself to everyone. He started out by saying he didn't feel Mary had anything serious. "She has a condition called angina. It can be extremely uncomfortable, and it feels very much like a heart attack. However, it's not life threatening, and it generally goes away by itself. The good news is she can put a tiny little pill of nitroglycerin under her tongue. It dissolves quickly and moments later the chest pain disappears."

Augie interrupted. "Excuse me doc, isn't nitroglycerin the stuff that's used in explosives?"

"Yep, it makes you wonder how someone came to discover it could be used to treat heart symptoms doesn't it?" Doctor Baime went on to say he wanted Mary to stay in the hospital until tomorrow for observation. "If you're feeling okay in the morning, you can get out of here." He added, "Mary, I suspect you don't get very much exercise. If it's possible, I'd like for someone to take you for a walk every day. Start out with short walks and gradually increase the distance. I'd be pleased if you can get to where you walk a mile or more each day. It would also help if you could take off some weight. I think you'll find that you'll feel better over all. Before he left he said, "It looks like you're rich with friends, Mary. That's great. It says a lot about you."

After doctor Baime left the room, Mary said, "What did Will have to say this morning?" Everyone laughed.

Leslie sat on the bed and took Mary's hand. "He called at two o'clock, but you already knew that, didn't you?" Leslie smoothed Mary's hair back. She gave Mary a brief account of their conversation.

"How did he sound?"

"He sounded very tired. I don't know if it was the telephone connection, or him. He sounded weak."

"It must have felt so good to hear his voice, and to know he's going to be coming home soon."

"I still can't believe it. I never gave up hoping, but there have been times when I thought I might never see him again. I've been afraid, if he didn't make it, we might never know what happened to him." Mary complimented her for being so strong. Leslie admitted she'd had lots of moments when she hadn't felt that way at all.

Mary smiled, "We don't realize our strength until we've managed to get past feeling so weak. Try not to be critical of yourself for having had those moments of weakness."

Thomas helped Leslie move Merlin's cage from his truck to the jeep. He patted her back." For what it's worth, Mary's spent a lot of sleepless nights worrying about Will. I've never seen her get so frustrated with herself. She's blamed herself because she wasn't always able to see what was going on with him. I think we've all felt helpless. Leslie thanked him for telling her that about Mary.

On the way to Norma's, Leslie found herself thinking seriously about what lay ahead. She'd managed to earn Merlin's trust and help him to heal physically. The role she'd played in his recovery had given her a sense of purpose. It had also helped to keep her hopes alive. Will's physical recovery was going to be up to others. She was mostly concerned with how, what he'd experienced was going to affect him emotionally. In his early letters home she saw him becoming increasingly bitter and cynical about the war. After a while he stopped criticizing what was going on. His correspondence switched to describing people in his unit, and his surroundings. She saw it as 'typical Will'. He'd decided he was feeling sorry for himself and he was making every effort to try to sound positive. She could imagine him saying something to the effect, 'pissing and moaning about it isn't going to change a thing. I need to put in my time, do what's expected of me and try not to let it screw up the rest of my life'. She could agree with those sentiments if they were real. For Will, she saw them as a way of trying to get through a painful negative experience. Maybe everyone thrown into traumatic circumstances had to suppress their emotional selves in order to survive. She wondered if anyone ever recovered from those kinds of devastating experiences completely.

Leslie turned off the main highway onto the county road that ran past Norma's place. She found herself thinking about how the events of these past few months had affected her. Even before Will had been captured she'd gone through bouts of acute anxiety and feeling depressed, fearing something bad would happen and she might never see him again. She didn't know how she'd ever be able to manage without him. She'd known him ever since fifth grade when her family moved into a house two doors over from where he lived. By the time the two of them entered junior high school together she had a crush on him. For his part, she was the girl next door, a casual friend. It wasn't until their sophomore year in high school he began to take notice of her. Until then it had been a one-sided fantasy relationship. She never thought he'd come to love her and they'd end up married.

The summer between their junior and senior year of high school, Leslie volunteered to accompany Will to the resort. Jeanne was undergoing aggressive cancer treatments that left her barely able to function. The two of them stepped in and ran the resort for the next several months. Leslie had all sorts of fears about not being up to the task. She'd felt overwhelmed starting out, but the experience had forced her to stretch herself and discover strengths she didn't know she had. She'd come away from it feeling much more self-assured. The events of the past few months had taken her to new levels of uncertainty and fear. She credited her family of friends, Norma and her devotion to saving Merlin to her emotional survival.

As she neared Norma's place she thought, *Will deserves a lot of credit. I've seen him go through all sorts of stuff over the years and he's somehow managed to rise above it. I can't think of a time when he's ever been critical of me or put me down. He's always been encouraging. In my weakest moments I've drawn strength from the examples he's set. We've been partners in the truest sense of the word."* As she pulled into Norma's place Merlin let out a screech. Leslie took it to mean he knew where he was, and he liked being here. She spoke to the hawk, "Merlin, I can hardly wait for you to meet Will. I wonder if either of you will sense the connection between you."

Chapter 12

After three days at the Army hospital in the Philippines, Will was flown to Hawaii where he underwent more testing. The infection in his leg wasn't showing any signs of improvement. The doctors began to wonder if he had something else wrong, or perhaps it was a bacteria that was resistant to the antibiotics that were available.

He went through an extensive, exhausting debriefing about his experience beginning with the orders he'd received for the mission his team had gone on. Over a period of a day and a half, he was questioned about what had gone wrong with the mission, his request for extraction, his capture, being rescued by the Hmong, and on and on. They even had questions about the time he'd spent with the psychiatrist, Colonel Bowen. Many of the questions didn't make sense to him. They seemed either inane or irrelevant. He repeatedly asked what some of the questions had to do with anything. By late into the first day he was becoming so exhausted he could barely be civil. He was especially perturbed by repeat questions. "Aren't you people listening? You've asked me the same fucking thing six times already." By late the next morning he told them he'd had enough. "I'm done. No more. When I'm up to it, I'll dictate a full account of what I can recall to a stenographer. I can't take anymore. You people are driving me crazy."

The door to the room opened. A short, wiry man with bottomless blue eyes stood in the doorway. When he stepped into the room everyone jumped up, stood at attention, and saluted. The General saluted tersely and approached Will. "How's it going Lieutenant?"

Will hesitated. A major said, "Sir, the Lieutenant is refusing to cooperate with this debriefing interview."

"Is that right, Lieutenant?"

"Yes sir," Will said, the muscles in his jaw tense.

"And why is that?" Will started to explain his physical condition. The General interrupted. "I'm aware of your injuries, Lieutenant." Will explained he wasn't refusing to cooperate, but many of the questions were redundant, or, in his opinion, irrelevant. He challenged his being questioned about his conversations with Dr. Bowen citing doctor/patient privilege. He gave examples of some of the questions he'd been asked.

"Sir, I'm tired. I'm not feeling well. I am not refusing to cooperate. I've been through a lot in the past few months. I don't think I should be forced to retell every detail of that experience, especially not now."

"I couldn't agree more, Lieutenant." He looked at the Major in charge. "I want a full transcript of the interview you've conducted up to this point on my desk by 0900 tomorrow. I also want a complete list of your questions. I'll review and edit them." He scrutinized each member of the team. "You're all dismissed."

After the interview panel was gone the General turned to Will. "I'm sorry, Lieutenant. I guarantee it won't happen again." The General pulled up a chair and sat down. "I didn't just happen by. There are two or three things I wanted to discuss with you." He took off his hat, and relaxed his posture somewhat. "First off, let me welcome you home. I'm aware of your having been captured, and your recent liberation. I'm also aware of your medical condition. You've indeed been through a lot." Will thanked him. "No Lieutenant, I'm the one who should be thanking you, which brings me to the second topic. By all accounts of the events that led to your capture, you've been nominated to receive the

Distinguished Service Cross, which is the highest honor awarded by the Army. Congratulations. There will be a formal ceremony at the appropriate time. That brings me to the third topic. You're going to be transferred to the Walter Reed Army hospital in Washington. Reed is considered the best of the Army's hospital facilities. As soon as you're situated at Reed the Army will transport your wife there. This experience has been an ordeal for her as well." Will closed his eyes for a moment. The General stood, and gave Will a reserved smile. "Dave Bowen, the psychiatrist you talked to, and I have been friends for years. He called me and asked if I'd look in on you. He's never done that before. I'm glad he did." The General reached out to shake Will's hand.

Two days later a military transport plane carrying Lieutenant Willis Morrissey arrived at Andrews Air Force base in Washington, D.C.. Will was transported directly to Walter Reed Army hospital. The doctors there had already scheduled him for surgery the next morning. The decision had been made to amputate his leg six inches below the knee. Will asked that he not undergo surgery until his wife could be present. One of the doctors seemed put-out with the delay saying, "What's the difference whether she's here or not. The leg has to be amputated. Let's just do it and get it over with."

Will looked at him and said. "You're fired."

The doctor looked at him in astonishment. "Excuse me, what did you just say?"

"You heard me. I said you're fired. I'm not letting you lay one Goddamn finger on me, and nothing is going to happen until my wife gets here. Please leave."

The doctor was irate and threatened to report Will to the hospital commandant. He'd never been treated this way by any patient before, and Will was about to find himself in a universe of trouble. As the doctor started for the door Will pointed his finger like a pistol at the doctor and pretended to shoot him. Two male nurses who were in the room at the time turned to one another. "Tyler, did you see or hear anything?"

"No. I believe Dr. Evil must have gotten out on the wrong side of the bed this morning. He sure seems to be in a foul mood." Tyler smiled broadly at Will. "That was outstanding, Lieutenant. I don't think he's all that good a doctor myself. You'd be much better off with Doc Schaeffer. Don't you think, Morgan? The other nurse agreed.

"Thanks guys. Don't stick your necks out on my account. I can stand up for myself. I just wish I could stand on both legs so I could kick his ass."

Tyler chuckled, "Lieutenant, I hope you intend to ask for a medical discharge. I don't think you're going to have a very bright future in this man's Army with that attitude."

"I don't have a very bright future as a one legged soldier anyhow. I figure the military owes me some medical care, kind of like workman's comp. After that, we'll go our separate ways."

Leslie arrived at the hospital late in the evening. Will was asleep when she came into his room. She stopped a few feet from the bed feeling a mixture of joy at seeing him and abject sorrow at how depleted he looked. He awakened but the room was dimly lit and he thought it was one of the nurses checking on him. "Will, it's me." She went to his bedside. "Can I hug you? I mean, is it okay."

He patted the bed and asked her to come sit next to him. They held one another. "God, Les, I thought I'd never see you again." Will asked her to turn on the lamp he wanted to see her.

She sat on the bed and touched his face. "Will, you've lost so much weight." He said the same about her. After all this time neither of them knew where to begin. Will commented about her letting her hair grow long again. She asked what had been decided about his leg. He told her it needed to be amputated. "Gangrene's set into the lower part." He invited her to pull the sheet aside to see for herself. "Oh, my God, Will. Did this happen the day you were captured?" He told her what he remembered about falling from the helicopter, and that his shoulder had been injured, too. She told him about she and Thomas finding Merlin the same day he'd gone missing and how similar the hawk's injuries were to his. He asked what Mary had to say about the likenesses? "You can probably guess the answer." She told him Mary saw the hawk as a kind of spirit messenger. It had come to them to let them know you'd been captured, you were injured and you came close to dying a couple of times."

Will changed the subject to ask about how Jeanne and Augie, and Thomas and Mary were doing. He asked if Feisty was done with his internship yet. He finally asked about his mother and brother. After she reported on everyone Leslie decided to tell him about his father's recent passing. Will's only comment was to say, "I'll bet he left my mother with nothing." Leslie told him his mother had insisted Ted take out some life insurance, but she didn't know how much the policy was for.

Leslie opted to stay with Will the rest of the night rather than leave to check into the guest dormitory. She had a number of questions she wanted to ask about how he'd managed to survive over the past five months. Augie had cautioned her not to press him about what he'd just been through. "There's a lot going on inside him, Leslie. He'll share what he can, when he can. It'll come out in bits and pieces. It's not that he doesn't trust you. It has nothing to do with you."

Will was lying on his back. He couldn't roll to either side without suffering pain. Leslie lay on her side next to him. "Will can I ask you one question." He nodded. "How long were you kept a prisoner?"

He told her he didn't really know. He told her he'd been unconscious for a prolonged period of time. "When I finally regained consciousness it took me a while to realize the bastards had abandoned me out there in the middle of the fucking jungle." He made no mention about the condition he was in when he came to. He told her about having been found by a group of Hmong people and taken to their hideout in the mountains. "I wouldn't have survived if it weren't for them. I'd have either starved to death or been eaten by something. I was in no shape to fend for myself." That brief explanation begged for dozens of more questions. He was starting to fidget.

Will underwent the surgery to remove his leg the second morning Leslie was there. The protruding tibia, the larger of the two bones in the lower leg had been shattered. The smaller one, the fibula had broken off more cleanly, but had jammed upward into the muscle tissue in the back of the leg. The doctors cut away all of the infected tissue. The muscle damage and the months of immobility of the leg left no question the leg needed to go. They considered removing the leg just above the knee, but decided that could be done later on if it proved necessary. He'd have greater mobility if he still had the knee joint.

Will was moved to a four-bed room in the medical wing that evening. Two of the beds were occupied by other soldiers. One of his roommates, Second Lieutenant, Donald Ackerman, had lost both of his legs to a land mine. He'd been amputated two weeks before. He conversed with Leslie while Will drifted in and out of sleep. The young lieutenant confessed to her that, as bad as losing his legs was, he was sure that he would have been killed had he remained in Nam. He told her a lot of lieutenants ended up being shot from behind, by their own men. This was news to her. Will had never mentioned anything about fratricide in his letters to her. She wondered if he'd done that on purpose to spare her any added worry. Ackerman didn't impress Leslie as a strong leader. She thought to herself, *even if he'd survived his year-long tour, he probably would have ended up a mental case. Maybe he will anyhow.*

She saw nothing of the other roommate who kept the privacy curtain surrounding his bed closed at all times. Whenever a nurse entered the closed-off space his few utterances were mostly unintelligible gibberish. Leslie could only make out a very few of his words. She wondered what had happened to him. On the third day Leslie encountered one of the nurses, and asked her about Will's other roommate.

"That's Sergeant Sullivan. He was severely burned when a mortar round blew up fuel barrels. He hasn't got a hair on his body. The most severe burns occurred to his upper body, his face and hands especially. He's been through hell during the almost nine months he's been here. He looks grotesque. That's why he keeps the curtains drawn. He doesn't want anyone to see him. His face was so badly burned his facial muscles are drawn back to either side. He looks like he's grinning all of the time, and he can't close his lips. That's why his speech is almost impossible to understand. There are several letters he can't pronounce. Think about it, letters like M or B or P. You can't pronounce those letters if you can't close your lips. To make it worse, it's painful for him to try to hold a pen to write because the skin is so tight and brittle. We apply lotions and ointments to him all the time. All that does is help to reduce the skin from splitting. The nurse lowered her voice. "The worst part of it all is, he hasn't had a visitor in all the time he's been here. Not one. I don't even know if he's got family anywhere. He couldn't tell us even if he does. He just sits there day in and day out by himself. The only people he has any contact with are the nursing staff and his doctors."

A couple of days later Leslie told Will about Sgt. Sullivan while they were strolling the hallway, Will in a wheel chair. He listened, "I wish there was something we could do for him, Will." When he made no comment, Leslie said, "This isn't like you. You're always ready to reach out to someone who needs help."

"It's not that, Les. I just think the poor guy's probably depressed as hell and tottering on the edge. I'm not sure what anyone can do for him. I'd hate to be the one to trigger his pulling the plug. He probably feels like he doesn't have a future, and there's only one way to end the suffering." Leslie looked at Will. "Did you feel that way after you were captured?"

Will looked away. She apologized feeling like she'd stepped way over the line. He finally said, "There was a point when I decided I couldn't go on the way I was, and I saw no hope of survival. The worst part was I was too weak to do anything." They turned around to start back to the room. "If the Hmong hadn't found me I probably would have died in two or three days anyway."

"Will, the big difference is, you were alone, there was no one. This man's not alone. He's surrounded by people willing to help."

"That's not the way he sees it. He's faced with a future of endless pain, and suffering and loneliness."

"Will, I can't accept that. Somebody has to at least try to help him."

"Look, Les, I don't know what to do. I'm in too fucking much pain myself to think straight." Will had never been that impatient or spoken that harshly to Leslie ever before. She looked dumbstruck. He immediately apologized.

Before they re-entered the room Leslie stopped. "Will, I realize you're in a lot of pain. I can't begin to imagine what you've been through. I'm scared. I want to help you but I need you to lead the way. I appreciate you telling me a little about what happened."

Two days after the amputation Will developed an infection in the stump. He'd hoped to be able to go home to recuperate and heal, but the doctors refused to release him until they were sure they had it under control. Leslie needed to return to Wisconsin. She'd made tentative arrangements with Feisty and Sunny for them to drive to D.C. and the four of them would return home together. She called them to postpone the trip indefinitely.

Lieutenant Ackerman had already been released. His parents had flown in from Iowa to take him back home. Will was able to dress himself by now. Leslie had gotten him some jeans, t-shirts and a pair of deck shoes. He could slip into the one easily. He half jokingly said he was going to look around for someone who had his left leg lopped off, and he'd give the other shoe to that guy. As it turned out he found such a person a couple of days later. The two of them exchanged shoes. Will began taking excursions. Short ones using crutches, longer ones in his wheel chair. He found a nice garden area not far from the wing he was in. He went there at least once a day to spend a couple of hours reading and people-watching.

Rather than taking meals in his room, he preferred eating in the central dinning room where he usually found a group of patients to converse with. He realized he was avoiding spending time in his room. He couldn't stop thinking about the things Leslie had said to him about his roommate, Sgt. Sullivan. One evening after dinner Will swiped a couple of plastic glasses and brought them back to the room. He opened one of the bottles of wine Leslie had managed to sneak in for him. He poured both glasses half full and managed to transport them to his bedside table. "Sgt. Sullivan, can I call you Tim?" There was no reply. "My wife Leslie brought me a bottle of wine. We enjoy having a glass or two or three in the evenings. Do you drink wine?" No sound. "Here, Tim, I poured some for you." Will wheeled himself over to the drawn curtain and slipped his hand inside of the curtain offering Tim the glass. Nothing happened. He decided to set the glass on the floor inside of the curtains. Still nothing happened. "Do you prefer beer? I don't have any, but maybe we can get one of the orderlies to sneak some in for us," still no response. "Excuse me Tim, I need to piss. I'll be right back." Will left to take care of business. When he returned he saw the glass had been picked up.

Will finished his wine. He waited a while; then he asked. "I'm going to have another glass. Would you like more?" No response.

"I've got an idea, Tim. How about we set up a little system of communication. Let's start out with this. When you want to say 'yes' to something, tap once. When you want to say 'no', tap twice. Okay?" Nothing happened. "Yo, Tim, do you want some more wine?" Still nothing happened.

"Hmm," Will considered. "Okay, let's add to our system. Three taps means, 'piss off, leave me alone'." Will immediately heard three taps. "Very good, Tim, that was eloquent, and your enunciation was perfect." Again there were three taps, only louder. "I'm sorry Tim, that was pretty sarcastic of me." A single tap. "So, can we start over?"

Would you like another glass of wine?" A moment

passed. There was a single tap and a hand set the glass on the floor outside of the curtain. Will took it and poured them each another. This time they were almost full. He reached inside the curtain and a hand took the glass from him.

"So Tim, you still haven't answered my question. Do you like this kind of wine?" There was no response. "Okay, let's add another one, four taps means I don't know. When you give me four taps, then I'll try to think of another question. Is that okay." Will heard a single tap. "Good, so do you like this kind of wine?" There were four taps. "You know what, Tim, I need to write our code down, and give you a copy. If we add many more responses we're not going to be able to keep track and we're going to get confused. We'll forget how many taps mean what. Is that okay?" A single tap. As Will transcribed the code he told Tim about where he'd been in Vietnam. Without saying why, he told Tim about having spent some time with some Hmong people. He asked if Tim had ever heard of them. Two taps.

"I hadn't either. The thing of it is, we couldn't understand a thing the other person was saying. I lived among them for over four months. We were never able to speak with one another, but we still managed to communicate using pantomime, pictures and gestures. I got to be kind of friends with a few of them. I miss them. I hope they're safe." There was silence. Will sipped his wine.

"I have another idea, Tim. Let's do this. When I ask you a question and I'm close to being right, can you say 'orn' for warm, if I'm not close, say 'old' for cold. Those are tongue sounds. Okay?" There was a single tap. "That's great, Tim. I know I'm a dumb fuck, but..." There was another single tap. "Very funny, Tim" Will waited. "Okay, here we go. I'm going to ask you where you're from. The way we're going to do this is, I'm going to give an area. You let me know if I'm 'orn' or 'old'. Are you from the east?" In a raspy voice he heard 'old'. "Are you from the west?" The response was 'old'. "Are you from the mid-west?" He heard 'orn'. This went on for a while and in time Will was able to determine that Tim was from Chicago, and from the south side of the city.

"No shit. I'm going to take a long-shot on this one, Tim. Would you by any chance happen to know a little guy by the name of Frank Noonan?" He heard a resounding single tap.

"Jesus," Will said. "I know you can't possibly know this, but Frank, I nick-named him 'Feisty' a few years ago, is my very best friend. He moved out to the suburbs when he was in seventh grade and we got to be friends back then. When I'm ready to leave here he and his wife and my wife, Leslie, are going to come here to take me back home to northern Wisconsin." Will immediately realized, in his enthusiasm, he'd said the wrong thing. He was saying 'goodbye, just as they were beginning to form a relationship.

"Hey, Tim, I'm sorry. Really, I am." He thought for a while. "Let's add a couple of more to the list. Five taps means 'okay', six means 'not okay'. After a few seconds Will heard five taps. Give me your sheet of paper so I can write those down. Tim handed the sheet out to him. "Let me ask, Tim. Do you still need to be here? What I mean is, could you leave this place, or do you still need medical attention?" There was no answer.

"Shit, I'm sorry that's two questions. Do you need to be here?" He heard four taps. "Are you going to need any more surgery?" Four taps. "Have they told you anything about future treatment?" Two taps. "Why not?" Four taps. "Are you ambulatory?" Four taps. Will thought for a moment. "Do you know what ambulatory means?" Two taps. "Let's add one more, Tim. Seven taps means 'I don't understand'," Five taps. "Ambulatory means able to get around on your own." One tap, and the sheet of paper reappeared. Will wrote down number seven.

Red-tailed Spirit Code System

one tap................Yes

two taps..............No

three taps............Piss off

four taps.............I don't know

five taps..............okay

six taps................not okay

seven taps...........I don't understand

eight taps............Incredible

nine taps.............Shut the f__k up

old = cold

orn = warm

Chapter 13

At 11:00 P.M. the shift changed. There was a tall black orderly named Sam who worked week-night shifts. Sam was well liked mostly because of his upbeat sense of humor. He joked around with the patients. Even though Tim never responded to Sam, that didn't stop Sam from 'jiving with Timothy'. When he came into the room that evening he greeted Will, "Hey, Will how you doing this fine evening?"

"Just fine, Sam." Will was sitting in one of the visitor's chairs.

"How come you're up so late and sitting in a chair?"

"I've been visiting with Tim."

"Yeah, right, and the two of you are leaving here tomorrow on a two week Caribbean cruise.

"Tim, Sam here doesn't believe me? Tell me, are you from New York?" Two taps. "Are you from Chicago?" One tap. "Are you from the south side?" One tap. "Where am I from?" Four taps.

"I'll be damned," Sam said. One tap. Will showed Sam the code sheet. Sam was delighted. "Timothy, my man, I am truly proud of both of you. This is ingenious. Will, here has figured out a way to converse with you, but I'm proudest of you. You took a chance and let him in." No response. "Hey, man, lets add another one. Number eight means, 'no shit man', 'I can't believe what I'm hearing'." Five taps. Sam said. "Hey Tim, I'm coming in to your sanctuary," five taps. "This is beautiful, Timothy, I can't believe what's happening here." Inside the curtains Sam attended to several things talking to Tim while he worked. Finally he said. "Tim, do you think we could open the curtain so you can meet Will face to face?" There was a long moment of silence. "Hey, what kind of cool aid are you boys drinking here tonight?" Sam laughed again. "Well that explains it. Will here gets you shit faced, and you turn into a babbling idiot." There was another brief moment, Timothy, my man, you got nothing to lose." Sam opened the curtain apparently without Tim's permission. Sam looked back and forth at Will and Tim. He introduced them to one another. Tim nodded to, Will. "Go shake hands with Will, Tim. He's not going to bite you."

Tim's entire head was badly scarred. He had a fixed expression that looked less like a smile, and more like a sardonic grin. His eyes, however, bore a look of apprehension. Because of the way his cheeks were drawn back, Tim's lips couldn't close, and his teeth were exposed. Tim reluctantly stepped forward. Will held eye contact with him. They shook hands, but Will didn't let go. Will put his other hand on top of Tim's and said in almost a whisper. "Welcome home, Tim." Tim stood half bent and he put his other hand on top of Will's. He nodded. Will asked, "Were you burned all over?"

Sam came over. He touched Tim's shoulder lightly and said to Will, "His worst burns are to his upper body. He had some less serious burns to the backs of his legs. It was pretty touch and go for almost four months with this good man. It's a damn miracle he made it at all." Sam looked at Tim and pulled Tim closer to him. "If anybody deserves a medal for bravery, it's this man right here. I know you hate me sayin' that, Tim, but it's the damn truth. There's a lot of sorry people in this hospital who've been through a lot, but none of them has been through what you have." Tim looked down.

"I think you're embarrassing Sgt. Sullivan," Will said to Sam. Tim made a single click sound with his tongue.

"That's okay," Sam said. "What I just said is the

damn truth, and I'm not going to apologize for saying it." He rubbed Tim's shoulder lightly. "So where's your stash of cool aid?" Sam asked.

Tim made three clicking sounds. Will laughed. "That's code for 'piss off,' we're not telling." Tim's cheeks raised slightly indicating an attempted smile.

"I have an idea," Will said. "Sam, is there a hat around here?"

"What kind of hat?"

"I don't care, just a hat; a baseball hat, how about a baseball hat?"

"I'll see what I can find. I'll be back in a few."

"Can you help me get into my wheel chair, Tim?" One click, and Tim wheeled the chair over to where Will was sitting. Tim held the chair while Will transferred himself into it. Sam came back into the room with an adjustable baseball hat that said 'Security' on it.

"Perfect." Will looked at Tim. "Put it on. There's a nice garden area down stairs. Let's take the elevator and go down there. It's a beautiful spring evening. Let's get out of here and enjoy some fresh air. Tim eyes showed fear, he gestured to his scarred arms and his face.

"I'll get you a shirt, Tim," Sam said, and he left again.

Tim shook his head and made the two click sound repeatedly. "Tim, it's after dark. The only people we're going to encounter are medical staff. You've got a hat. Sam's getting you a shirt. You've been cooped up in this fucking room for months. Come on, the two of us are going to go down to the garden. But first, you need to pour some more wine." He pointed to the closet. "The wine's in there. There's a cork screw in my jacket pocket." Tim looked at Will searchingly. Will held out his hand. "Tim, we've both been through a lot. We need to help one another." Tim held up his glass, waved his hand over it and tapped on it twice. He was refusing anything more to drink. "I understand. There's a part of me that wants to get shit-faced and just stay that way." Tim nodded his understanding.

Sam returned with a hooded sweatshirt. "I borrowed this from lost and found. If it fits, it's yours, Tim." He helped Tim on with it. It was large on him. "That's okay, Timothy. You'll grow into it." Tim wheeled Will down the hall, into the elevator and out to the garden area. Tim took several deep breaths.

The garden area was softly illuminated. It was a warm evening. Will propped his left leg on the bench. Tim sat down facing him. They sat there for a while savoring the garden and the evening. "I don't know why Tim, but I just had a recollection of a particular night back in Nam. I was in really bad shape, and I was by myself in the jungle. There was no moon. The jungle was so dense I couldn't even see any stars. It was like being in a sensory deprivation chamber. I'd never experienced such complete darkness. All of a sudden I caught a flash of light. A few seconds later I saw it again, and then again. It was fucking fireflies, I couldn't believe it. Here I was halfway around the world, and there were fireflies. I know it sounds crazy, but those stupid bugs helped me feel less alone and miserable." Tim's eyes had a look of complete understanding.

"Christ," Will said. "I forget, you grew up in the city. Did you ever see fireflies as a kid?" Tim nodded and clicked once. "Isn't it amazing what such a little thing like that can do to get you through?" Tim nodded again and he gestured expansively to the garden.

The next day Leslie called early in the morning. He told her he'd met his other roommate, Tim Sullivan. "Les, you're not going to believe this. It turns out Tim grew up on the south side of Chicago and he knows Feisty. What are the odds of that?"

She told him Feisty and Sunny were up for the weekend, but they weren't there at the moment. They'd gone to look at a piece of property. She'd ask if Feisty remembered Tim. "Will, what's happening with the infection?"

"I don't know. The doctors aren't saying much. I don't think they've seen this strain of bacteria before." He told her he'd finally figured something out." He told her about the medicine man and him putting what Will thought was rice on the infected part of his leg. "It wasn't rice. I think he was putting maggots on the wound. The maggots were feasting on the bacteria that were causing the infection. That's what kept the gangrene from spreading." Leslie seemed skeptical. She asked if he'd presented that theory to any of his doctors. "Not yet, but I will."

When Dr. Schaeffer came in to examine Will's leg that morning. Will asked if he could have a few minutes with him privately. Schaeffer wheeled him down the hall into a conference room.

Will explained what had happened between Tim Sullivan and him last night. "I've got a couple of questions, Doc. Is there anything that can be done to help him be able to close his mouth. He can't speak because the skin's so tight. The same thing is true for his hands. He can't even hold a pen or make a fist. Dr. Schaeffer reminded Will he wasn't Tim's doctor, and that he was an orthopedic surgeon, not a dermatologist or a plastic surgeon, he wasn't qualified to speak to Tim's situation. "I know, but you carry some weight around here, and you give a damn. I think whoever's treating him has given up on him. Dr. Schaeffer excused himself, telling Will he'd be right back. When he returned he was accompanied by the nursing supervisor for that unit, Carol Bradly.

She had Tim's charts with her. She said the orderly on duty last night had put Tim's chart on her desk with a note asking her to please read his entry. She said she was amazed when she'd read it. She gave Dr. Schaeffer a brief summary of Tim's injuries and his present condition. The pained expression on Schaeffer's face made it clear he was willing to see what could be done to help Tim. He asked if Tim had been evaluated by a plastic surgeon. Carol told him Tim had been seen by two of them about three months ago. "They said that as soon as Tim was completely healed they could begin a series of skin grafts that would relieve a lot of the tension in both his face and hands.

She addressed both Will and Dr. Schaeffer. "A big part of the problem is that Tim has withdrawn from everyone and everything. He's refused to cooperate with any recommendations for further treatment of any kind. It's like he's given up on himself." She hesitated before saying, "I think he just wants to die."

"I understand that," Will said. "I've been there." He paused, "Let me ask. If he were to consent to going through this 'series' of grafting procedures, how long would it take, and how much is it going to improve his ability to function?"

Bradly didn't know the answer to Will's first question. "The plastic surgeon will be the one to ask. It's going to involve a lot of pain, but we can manage that. The fact is, he's in constant pain the way he is. He'll feel a lot better once the tension is relieved. As for whether it will improve his ability to function, a lot of that will depend on Tim. It will allow him to talk and use his hands. He's going to have to work at making those things happen." Will asked if anyone would object to him trying to talk Tim into giving it a shot.

"I have no objection, Will. We'd all be thrilled if you're able to get through to him. He's built up some formidable walls." She hesitated, "The danger is, Tim has 'a very low disappointment threshold'. He's afraid to hope for anything. Surgery can reduce, maybe even eliminate, his pain. It can certainly help him become more functional. Some of his scars can even be removed or at least made less ghastly looking. He's extremely self-conscious about his appearance. He views himself as being some kind of monstrous freak." Will was aware of that. He described the lengths he and Sam had gone to get Tim to go out to the garden last night.

Nurse Bradly asked Will, "What happens if Tim refuses? How's that going to affect you? "

"I can't answer that." Will looked down. Then he looked at her again. "This is going to sound calloused, but I guess my feeling about him is, he hasn't got a life. He might as well be dead than to go on like this."

Bradly said if Tim was willing to give it a try, she'd put in a request for him to be reevaluated by one of their plastic surgeons. She was familiar with an occupational therapist on staff who she regarded as outstanding. She wanted her to evaluate Tim as well.

As Will started to leave, Bradly said, "In case you weren't aware of it. There is a solarium on the top floor. It's a nice place to enjoy a view of the campus, and relax when the weather's bad.

When Will returned to the room a nurse was rubbing lotion on Tim's back. He wheeled himself up to Tim's bed. Tim was lying in a prone position in just his boxer shorts. Will looked closely at the rope-like scars on Tim's back, and asked the nurse, "How come his back looks like someone lashed him with a whip?"

"It's called 'keloiding'. It's fairly common with people who've suffered severe burns. It's even more pronounced on his chest and shoulders. Black people are especially prone to it."

"Does it hurt?" Tim rapped once. The nurse wasn't aware of their newly devised system of communicating.

"You'll have to ask Tim. His skin's not very elastic, so movement that stretches the skin hurts. He's also temperature sensitive to heat and especially cold. He also doesn't sweat like a normal person, so he has to avoid hot humid situations. Most of the sweat glands in his upper body were destroyed. His air conditioning system is barely working."

"Christ Tim, that means you won't be able to go back to Vietnam. Too bad for you." Tim rapped three times. Will watched as the nurse applied the lotion. "How often does he need to have that stuff put on?"

"In the summer, a couple of times a day," she explained. "More often in the winter, when the air is drier." She finished with his back. "Tim can do his front." She tapped his butt. "All done, Timothy."

"Ank ou," Tim said in his gravelly voice.

"Did the fire make your voice that way, too, Tim?" One rap.

"What's the tapping about," the nurse asked.

"We've developed a little code. One click means yes, two no, and so on."

"What's three clicks mean."

"You don't want to know."

"I want to know even more now."

"ell er," Tim said as he lifted himself to a sitting position.

"It means piss-off, leave me alone."

The nurse laughed. "I love it. I'm going to start using it."

"So, what about Tim's voice, you didn't answer my question?"

The nurse's smile disappeared. "The heat from the fire scorched his vocal chords, also. His operatic days are over." She put Tim's lotions on his bed stand. "See you guys later."

Tim sat on the edge of the bed holding a jar of lotion in one hand, applying it to the grotesque scar tissue with the other. Will studied the tangle of flesh. "The keloided skin is mostly on your shoulders, chest and upper back." Will observed. "Is that where the burns were the worst, or is that just where the keloiding occurred the most. Tim gestured to his face and the front of his upper body. "Urst urns."

"The worst burns," Will said. Tim nodded.

"I was just talking to the nursing supervisor. She told me that there's a solarium upstairs on the top floor. How about us going upstairs later on to check it out? Tim looked at Will with a dull expression in his eyes. Will read the meaning and said, "You want to wait until tonight when no one's around." Tim nodded.

He waited then addressed Tim. "I hope you're not going to get all pissed off with me, Tim. One of the reasons I was talking with the nursing supervisor was to ask about having a plastic surgeon take a look at you. Maybe they can graft some skin on either side of your face to relieve the tension so that you can close your mouth. You might be able to..."

Tim rolled his eyes, made a slashing gesture across his neck and pantomimed throwing his head away. He sat fuming. Will showed a wry smile, "I thought we might try the skin grafting first." Tim's expression softened, he looked down and shook his head. "Look, Tim, I know you've about given up. I just think it's worth at least looking at. If the surgeon says it can't be done, then that's that. If he thinks there's a possibility it can work, then we can decide whether to try it or not." Tim's expression hardened again. He pointed at himself exaggeratedly. Then he gestured back and fourth between Will and himself and he made a chopping gesture between the two of them, and pointed to himself again. "I get it," Will said. "It's not 'we', it's not us. It's your decision." Tim nodded as emphatically as he could.

"You're right, Tim. I'm sorry. That was damn presumptuous of me." Tim rapped once. "I need to choose my words more carefully. You're right, it is your decision." Tim clicked five times. His eyes softened again. "Here's a simple yes or no question, Tim. Would you be willing to let a plastic surgeon examine you to at least get an opinion?"

Tim looked up at the ceiling for a long moment, when he returned his gaze to Will he gave five clicks. "Great Tim," Will smiled. "That's all I'm asking, just give yourself a chance."

The same nurse from before came in to bring Tim and Will some fresh water. She helped Tim on with a loose t-shirt. "It's hard for him to put on and take off t-shirts. It stretches his scars to where they hurt." Will appreciated her explanation.

After the nurse left the room, he said. "There's one other thing, Tim. The supervisor also said that there is an occupational therapist on staff she'd like you to see. There are some things she might be able to help you with." Tim pointed his finger at Will as if to shoot him. "Is that a different way of saying 'yes'?" Tim shook his head.

"Come on. Make yourself decent, and lets go see Bradly and get the ball rolling."

Chapter 14

Will helped him on with the sweatshirt. Tim draped a towel over his head before donning his hat. "Christ, Tim, you look like Lawrence of Washington." He gave a slight laugh as he began wheeling Will toward the nursing supervisor's office. Will knocked on her door and she looked up from her desk and greeted Will. She squinted at Tim. "I'll be damned. Tim? Is that you?" She stood and invited them in.

"We just dropped by to let you know Tim's agreed to let himself be evaluated by a plastic surgeon, and to see the occupational therapist you mentioned."

"That's wonderful. I'll get going on it today. You've made my day, Tim. The whole staff is going to be thrilled." As they were about to leave she said, "I took the liberty of talking to Cathy, the occupational therapist I mentioned to you, Will. She said she could see Tim this afternoon." Will thanked her. On the way back to their room Will told Tim what an occupational therapist was, and what she might be able to do for him. When they got to the room Tim sat down on his bed and looked out the window.

"Tim, I know you're scared. There's a lot coming at you all at once. I wish we could talk about it." Tim turned to Will and put a finger to his lips as if to say, 'Be quiet'. Will nodded, "Okay, that's number 9, 'shut the fuck up'." Tim rapped once and gave Will a thumbs-up for getting the message.

That afternoon a short, plump lady came into the room. She had a great smile and beautiful blue eyes. "Hi, I'm Cathy D'Marco. I'm the OT Carol requested."

Will asked Tim if it would be all right if he sat in while Cathy interviewed him. Tim was agreeable. Cathy explained she was going to evaluate him to see what sorts of things she might come up with that would make life easier for him. She was already aware of the extent of Tim's injuries, and his speech limitations. She started out with having him try to hold a pen. He couldn't. "This is your lucky day," she reached into a large cloth bag and produced a pencil that was at least a half-inch in diameter. Tim could just barely manage to hold it. She reached into her bag again. She came up with a roll of thin foam rubber, a pair of scissors, and some friction tape. She wrapped the foam rubber around the pencil and had Will hold the foam in place while she taped it. Tim could hold it easily. "Okay, Tim" She extracted a tablet of lined penmanship paper, "Write me a note," Tim clicked four times.

Will explained the code to Cathy. "Four clicks means, 'I don't know'. Will showed her the code sheet. "Hey you guys, this is brilliant. I never would have thought of doing something like this. I especially like number three." Will hadn't written number 9 down yet.

"Everybody does." Will smiled.

Tim wrote his first words. "After all this time, I don't know what to say. Thank you, Cathy. Thank you, Will."

"Okay Tim, we're on our way. I'm going to take some of your clothes with me today. We can have Velcro sewn into your shirts and pants so you don't have to screw around with buttons and zippers any more. I'm going to get you fitted with a toupee. What color hair do you want?" Tim looked at her, and clicked four times. What color was your hair before?" She had to remind him he could write it down. He scrawled 'RED'. "Do you want red hair again?" Tim nodded. "Then red it will be. Red-red or dark auburn red?" Tim wrote 'bright red, they used to call me Rusty'. "Would you and Will come down to the OT clinic tomorrow. We'll measure you for the wig. We can have it for you in a couple of days.

Before leaving Cathy said. "I'll get you more tablets, Tim. I have a feeling you have lots to say." At the door she turned and made three clicking sounds with her tongue, "I love it. You guys are going to be fun to work with." She dropped by later that day to deliver the tablets and some toy clickers that looked like crickets and gave off a sharp sound. By the end of the week most of the staff was going around making clicking sounds. Number three and nine were their favorites.

Leslie called every day. She was delighted to hear about what was happening with Tim. She always called from the resort so Augie and Jeanne and Thomas, if he was there, could talk to Will." God, Will, it is so good to hear your voice," Augie said. "We've missed you. We can't wait till you get home." When Jeanne got on the line she began crying so hard she could barely carry on a conversation. Before hanging up she said, "Say 'hi' to Gabe." Let me hold the receiver close to his ear. Will greeted the dog. Gabe gave his single bark. The sound of it nearly brought him to tears.

Leslie and Sunny planned to leave for Washington a week before Memorial Day. Will was informed a few days earlier that an award ceremony was planned for Memorial Day at Walter Reed. Will was to be awarded the Distinguished Service Cross and a Purple Heart. Leslie offered to rearrange the travel plans to be there for the ceremony. "Les, it's not that important. I really don't want a stupid medal. I'd much rather that they just give me my discharge papers." She insisted. She wanted to be there for the ceremony.

The next day Will was fitted with a dress uniform. A captain from the Pentagon visited him to go over the details of the presentation. Since there was a little over a year left of his enlistment the officer spoke with him about reassigning him. He noted that Will was undoubtedly going to require several months to complete his recuperation, be fitted with a prosthetic leg and adjust to using it.

Will was curious. He asked, "Considering my injuries and the time it's going to take for my rehab, I'd think the Army would be glad to be rid of me."

"I've reviewed your combat records, Lieutenant. You've served this Nation well. That's why you're about to receive the Army's highest commendation. I'm sure, once you recover from the ordeal you've endured, your determination to serve your nation and its cause will be rekindled." As soon as the captain left the room Will gave three clicks. Tim made some 'huh' sounds. It was the closest he could come to laughing aloud.

Later that day Cathy came into the room to present Tim with a toupee. It was red all right. Cathy put it on him and fussed with adjusting it just so. She handed Tim a mirror. "Christ, Tim, that makes a big difference. What do you think?"

Tim wrote, "It makes me look like Howdy Doody."

Will laughed, "Yeah, the color boarders on garish." Cathy burst into laughter. She agreed and asked if it was too, red. Tim suggested making one the color of Will's hair. His red-head days were a thing of the past. He and Will exchanged glances. That could be said of a lot of things for both of them. He asked Cathy to help him on with his sweatshirt. After she left the two of them went for a walk. Will had built up enough stamina to make it to the garden area and back using his crutches. They sat in the garden for a while. Will finally said, "I don't know what's wrong with me, Tim. I can't help it. I'm feeling sorry for myself. I don't know whether I'm depressed or mad as hell." Tim wrote, 'Me too. It's both'. "I don't want any Goddamn medal. I'm not a hero. I got my ass shot out of a helicopter. There were people who risked their lives to save me. They're the heroes."

Tim wrote, 'tell me about them.' Will spent the better part of an hour recounting how he'd been found and taken care of by the group of Hmong people. He talked about their hideout in the mountains, and them eventually coming under siege by the VC. He left out his part in helping to defend their enclave. Tim was fascinated by Will's accounts of the 'medicine-man'. He was relieved to hear the Hmong people had managed to escape. Will avoided telling him about the napalm air strike for obvious reasons.

When they returned to their room, the door was closed. A nurse came up to them from behind. "Hey guys, you have a new roommate. His name is Private Clarence Teamore. He just got here today from Manila. He's sleeping right now." Will asked if Teamore was badly hurt. "He lost his left eye and his face and left arm caught a bunch of shrapnel. They did a hell of a job cleaning up his wounds in the Philippines. He's on a lot of pain meds."

For the next couple of days Will and Tim spent time away from the room to avoid disturbing Private Teamore. The Private slept a lot. At night he would wake up moaning. Will would summon a nurse to request more pain medication for him.

A couple of days went by before PFC Teamore was able to 'sit up. He had his first solid meal since before he'd been wounded. He had trouble chewing but he managed the eggs and oatmeal. He spoke with a pronounced southern accent revealing he was from a small town in southwest Mississippi, what he called 'Mississippi delta country'. Tim had never been there but he was familiar with several of the blues musicians and the music that came from that region. The left side of Pvt. Teamore's face was heavily bandaged. So was his left shoulder and neck. He said that the soldier next to him tripped a booby-trapped grenade. The other soldier was killed almost instantly. Clarence said he, himself, only had one week to go before his tour was over. "Shit man, ah guess ma luck jus run out a lil too soon. De tells me ma eye is done wit. I show doan know what I's gonna do wit myself now."

Will thought to himself, 'A person could make a career out of being an advocate, for guys like Clarence, and Tim. They don't know what to ask for, or what's available to help them to put their lives back together'. As he considered their situation he began to look at his own. He'd decided as early as junior high school that he wanted to be a teacher someday. He seriously doubted that would ever happen now. He wasn't ready to start thinking about his future. *I just want to get back to the lake and put all of this as far behind me as possible. I need a long vacation from the world. I just want to be with Les, and my family of friends, and old Gabe.*

He looked over at Tim who'd finished his breakfast and looked like he was writing something. *I can't leave Tim behind. Maybe I can persuade him to come with us. What's going to happen to him when it comes time for him to leave here?* Will got to his crutches and made his way over to where Tim sat. He plopped himself down next to him. "What's happenin'?" Tim showed Will a pencil drawing he was working on. "Jesus, Tim, I didn't know you could draw." Will took the note pad from him. It was a drawing of Will. Where did you learn to draw like this? Tim shrugged. "Tim, I want to show this to Cathy when it's done. Maybe she can fix you up with some decent paper and pencils. Do you know how to paint?" Tim shrugged again. Will showed the drawing to Clarence and the nurse who'd just come in the room. Both of them liked it. She said, "Tim, this looks just like a picture." She immediately realized how ridiculous the statement sounded. "No, what I mean is, this is almost like a photograph." She looked at Will, "don't even make one of your smart-assed remarks, Lieutenant. "

Will and Tim persuaded Clarence to go with them to the garden. It was a sunny warm day. Will wore a t-shirt and shorts and Tim was wearing his security hat and light blue scrubs. They got some scrubs for Clarence, too. They found a bench in a shaded area of the garden. Clarence was talking about how, having come from the Mississippi delta area, he hadn't had any problem adjusting to the heat and humidity in Vietnam. The monsoon season was another story.

Will happened to glance over and he did a double take. He couldn't believe what he was seeing. It was Leslie accompanied by Augie and Jeanne. "Oh my, God."

Jeanne embraced him unable to hold back her tears, "Oh, Will, it's so good to see you. I'm sorry, I promised myself I wasn't going to do this."

Augie was next-in-line and he gave Will a prolonged hug. "You look like you've lost a lot of weight, Will. You look leaner than when you went out for wrestling as a sophomore."

Will asked how come they were here, "I mean, how were you able to get away from the resort. Who's running the place in your absence?"

"Sunny and Feisty came up for a long weekend. Jeanne hired two ladies from nearby to help out with cleaning the cabins. It's gotten to be too much for us. Even with Leslie's help, we just run ourselves ragged every weekend. We're both wondering why we didn't do it sooner."

Leslie approached Tim. "Will told me about the code you two worked out." Tim nodded. He studied her expecting her to be repulsed by his appearance. "I'm glad he reached out to you, Tim." He just looked at her. After Will introduced everyone, Clarence suggested he and Tim head back to the unit. It was nearing lunchtime.

The rest of them stayed on in the garden. Leslie asked Will if there was any improvement with the infection in his stump. "I saw an infectious disease specialist on Wednesday. He put me on a couple of new antibiotics. It's too soon to tell. It doesn't seem to hurt as much." They knew about the award ceremony scheduled for the coming Monday, Memorial Day, and that Will would be one of the recipients. It was the main reason for them making the surprise trip.

Augie asked if there was a cafeteria where they could get some lunch. As Will led the way Augie asked questions about the hospital and the quality of care Will was receiving. Will sensed he was concerned about the decision to remove Will's leg and the fact that he now had a serious infection. "The leg had to come off, Augie. It probably could have been saved if I'd gotten medical attention early on." He shared Augie's skepticism about the subsequent infection following the amputation. Will gave Augie an abridged account of his rescue by the Hmong. He talked about the medicine man. Augie was astonished to learn the man had used maggots to treat Will's infection.

The topic of Tim came up during lunch. Will was wrestling with himself about Tim. If Tim underwent a series of plastic surgeries, Will wanted to stick around to be here for him. He also wanted to invite Tim to come stay with them in Wisconsin after the surgeries. He hadn't discussed either of those things with Leslie. If she objected he was prepared to remind her she was the one who'd practically insisted Will reach out to Tim. He realized he was feeling preemptively defensive. He was struggling with all sorts of ambivalent feelings. A part of him just wanted to retreat from the world. He wasn't sure he was up to the task of helping anyone when he was on such shaky ground himself. On the other hand, he knew he couldn't turn his back on Tim. If he did and it led to Tim committing suicide, he'd never be able to live with himself. He'd considered from the very start that might eventually happen anyway. It wouldn't take much of a disappointment for Tim to just say 'screw-it' and give up.

Augie asked if there was anything that could be done for Tim so he could speak again, and have some facial expression. Will told him they were working on it. He'd gotten Tim to agree to allow himself to be evaluated by a plastic surgeon. Augie had noticed Will was slowing down on their way to the cafeteria. He asked if Will had a wheel chair and if so, where was it. Will told him it was back in his room. Leslie said she'd go get it. She could see he'd pushed himself beyond his limits. Jeanne went along with her.

After they left, Augie brought up the pending commendation ceremony. "It's bullshit, Augie. I managed to survive. What's heroic about that?"

"From what I've been told, you stayed behind in order to hold off the enemy. That gave your men the time they needed to make it to the chopper. If you'd accompanied them, all of you might have been killed before you reached it. The chopper and it's crew may have gone down too. That sounds pretty heroic to me." Will had no response. All he remembered about what happened that day was almost making it into the chopper, trying to hang onto the landing rail and falling. Augie's statement jarred a buried memory loose. In the heat of the moment he'd reverted to pure instinct. For the first time Will recalled that, before starting for the hovering chopper, he'd thrown his two grenades. Then he'd emptied three or four clips at oncoming VC. He remembered struggling his way through the tall wet grass, having his helmet knocked off his head by a bullet and actually making it partway into the chopper. *Jesus, what else do I not remember? Maybe I wasn't unconscious the entire time I was held prisoner.* He remembered a second cage in the encampment. *Did the VC manage to get one of the others, too?* Augie asked if Will was okay.

"Yeah, it's just that I don't remember much about what happened that day. Who told you about it and what I did."

Augie had a one-word answer, "Mary." He went on to say he'd also been able to talk to one of the people who'd debriefed the men from his unit. "They all said the same thing, none of them thought they would have made it if you hadn't managed to hold the VC off."

Chapter 15

Will was beginning to perspire in his dress uniform as he sat in his wheel chair awaiting the awards ceremony to begin. He remembered back to his high school graduation. Feisty had taken off for the resort a few days earlier saying, 'Screw it, they can send me the diploma, I'm not sitting on those miserable folding chairs and sweat my ass off in a hot stinky gym'. Will was wishing he had the chutzpah or a good excuse not to be here for this. He was beginning to feel queasy like he was about to pass out when a four star General walked to the Center of the Stage, and a military band struck up the National Anthem. All of the military personnel stood at attention saluting as a color guard came down the center aisle. Will guessed there were close to two hundred people in the audience. He was able to locate Augie and Jeanne. Leslie was sitting between Clarence and Tim.

The General was the keynote speaker. He started out by saying, "We're here today not only to commemorate those who've given the ultimate sacrifice for this country, but to honor these brave men assembled here on this stage." He turned and gestured to the five men sitting behind him. He began his speech by acknowledging there was a growing objection to the war. He praised the courage and dedication of those who were serving despite the ridicule the mission was receiving. Will wanted to leave. The General paused and looked out over the audience. "After much soul searching I've decided I want and need to talk about something personal today. I've spent my entire adult life in the military. A soldier doesn't question orders or challenge the decisions that lead to War. It's our job to fight to win. That's what I've always believed." The General looked down. When he looked up again, he appeared to be struggling for composure. He bit his lip. "Two days ago we learned our oldest grandson was killed in action." A hush came over the entire audience. "Today, for the first time, I'm asking myself what this is all about. I've served this country in France and in Germany during World War II and as a senior officer of an infantry division in Korea. I know about the horror of war. Looking back, Korea doesn't make much sense to me anymore. I thought it did at the time. Today we appear to be engaged in another Korea. I'm in awe of these brave young men sitting here today," He turned to the five honorees. "I'm in awe of them because they went off to do what's become a thankless job. A large majority of people in this country are insisting we get out of Vietnam, that we never should have gotten involved there in the first place. These men went there and did the best they could. They survived and are here today because each one of them risked their lives to save others. Out there in the jungles it isn't about flags or anthems or ideologies. It's about the guy next to you. It's about trying to keep one another alive." He paused, "Two days ago I rediscovered something I guess I've always known. It's also about family sacrifice. If you walk through any of the buildings on this campus, you'll see many hundreds of men whose injuries are a testament to the brutality of war. Most of you in the audience today are family members or friends. I want to acknowledge the sacrifices you've made, too." He went on, "Today my faith is being tested. I can't tell you what the outcome will be. Soldiers coming home today feel they have to take off their uniforms, lest they be ridiculed on the streets as 'baby killers', as murderers who've committed genocide. I'm sure most of them just want to blend-in, and become a part of the woodwork." He shook his head. "That's sad." He paused. "For me, this war has become a very personal tragedy. I feel for all of you." He turned to the five recipients and welcomed them home.

Without further ado, the General presented each of the five recipients with their medals explaining what each of the soldiers had done to earn this recognition. Will was the third in line. After the General presented each recipient with his commendation, he shook hands, saluted, and made some personal comment to the soldier. When he came to Will he asked, "Lieutenant, are they taking good care of you?"

"Yes, sir." Will hesitated, "I'm sorry about your grandson, sir." The general thanked him.

Will could hardly wait to get back to the ward and strip out of his dress uniform. On the way Tea thanked Will for inviting him to the ceremony. He praised the general's speech saying he hoped the general wasn't going to get in trouble for some of the things he'd said. He was really sorry about the general's grandson. Tim wrote Will a note. 'Why didn't you tell me about being captured'?

"It must have slipped my mind."

Will asked Tea how he was doing. He told Will he was beginning to hurt. He said he was going to write his 'mama' to tell her about the ceremony. He was quiet for a few moments before saying, even though he was 'messed up' he was glad he'd made it back.

Will patted Tea. "You're a good man, Clarence. Welcome home." He took the medal he'd received off, looked at it and put it in his nightstand drawer.

Tim watched Will and wrote, 'Keep it. You've earned it.'

"Maybe, I don't know."

Will spent that evening with Augie, Jeanne, and Leslie. After dinner at a small Italian restaurant they went for a stroll on a promenade overlooking the Potomac river. Augie pushed Will in his wheelchair. Something about the evening inspired Leslie to ask Will, "Do you remember that evening when you, me and Feisty took Emil Bergstrom's boat and we drifted down the river together? None of us spoke a word. We just watched the sunset. I was so glad to see both of you. You'd just gotten back from a summer at the resort." She paused, "We talked about taking the boat up the river in the fall to see the colors, but we never did." Will asked what ever happened to that old boat. "It was still leaning up against the back of my parent's garage when we moved."

Leslie took his hand and Will squeezed and kissed it. After a while he said, "I appreciate what the general said about family sacrifices. I've thought a lot about what people must go through not knowing if a loved one is alive or not. They must live in constant fear."

Augie said, "We had Mary to rely on to tell us if you were still alive. There were a few times she wasn't sure you were going to make it. We worried constantly about your physical condition." What he didn't say was, they still did. Will experienced a brief flashback to when he discovered he'd been left in a cage and abandoned in the jungle. He'd had low moments in his life, but nothing like that.

Augie and Jeanne stopped by the hospital the next morning before leaving for the airport. Will seemed cheerful. He reported the Occupational Therapist, Cathy, had been in already to present Tim with a whole bunch of art supplies. She'd given him sketch pads and pencils as well as watercolor paints, brushes and paper. She'd also arranged for Tim to get some lessons in watercolor painting starting this afternoon. "She's managed to recruit some artists who volunteer their time to teach here." Will turned to Tim and said. "Jeanne's gotten really good at watercolors. I'm sure she and her artist friend Gloria can help you with it if you decide you like it." Tim and Leslie both looked at Will, and he instantly realized he'd just slipped, and given away his plan for Tim to come home with them. As soon as Augie and Jeanne left, he asked Tim and Leslie to take a walk with him. Outside the room Will said, "Tim, Les and I've been talking. We'd like to invite you to come back to Wisconsin with us." Tim looked back and forth between them as if to verify they were in agreement. Will stopped. "Tim, I don't know what your situation is, I mean about family, or home. The staff here say you haven't had a visitor in all the time you've been here." Tim looked away down the hall. "Look, Tim, it appears you're stuck here. You haven't got any other place to go. We'd like you to consider the offer. If you get there and find you don't like it, you don't have to stay." Will got a less serious expression, "Of course, I can't imagine anybody with even a scintilla of sense not liking it. I realize that the beauty and the serenity of the lake and the forests and having lively conversations with bright congenial people such as myself and Les may not appeal to a lot of people."

Tim wrote on his pad. "What about the plastic surgery? That's going to take some time. What will I do when I get there? What will I do for money?"

"Tim, you can stay at our place. We have a spare room. If you decide you like it and you want to stay, we can put up a place for you. It would be your own. Feisty and I have built several year-around cabins for Augie over the years."

"How would I get around?"

"I've got two vehicles, a jeep, and a pick up truck, and Leslie has a car. You could use one of those."

"I never learned to drive."

"You can learn. We'll teach you. Come on, Tim. What have you got to lose?"

Tim made four clicks meaning he didn't know. He wrote, "I need to think about it." Then he wrote, "When were you going to ask me?"

"Today. Les and I have talked about it. I was just waiting until she was here so we could present the idea together." Tim looked at her. She was smiling at Will. "Come on, Tim. Christ it's a new beginning for both of us."

He wrote. "Mother's dead. Father's an alcoholic. I don't know if he's still alive." He looked at Will.

"You know what Tim, we can't choose our families. You can't refuse this opportunity. If you do, Noonan and I will kidnap you."

Tim wrote. "Money, I need to pay my own way."

"I'm sure you're eligible for some kind of disability." Tim made four clicks. "Well, let's go find out. I need to find out what mine's going to be, too. We can figure out something, once we know how much you're getting. I've seen how little you eat. Our biggest expense is going to be wine."

Tim went to get his hat and towel. Leslie looked at Will. "We talked about the possibility of inviting Tim to come back with us. I didn't think WE'D reached a definite decision." She shook her head, "I agree with your decision, Will. It's just that you caught me by surprise." He apologized.

They got directions from the nursing supervisor to where the financial services office was. They found out Tim had continued to receive his monthly service pay plus four hundred a month in disability benefits. Once he was discharged he could apply for disability through the VA. They estimated he'd be eligible to receive just under a thousand dollars a month. He currently had close to twenty thousand dollars in his account. Tim tapped eight times. The paperwork for Will wasn't complete, but he'd continued to receive his service pay including the combat bonus. His account showed a balance of twelve thousand.

A few minutes after they got back to their room a heavy-set man in a white lab coat came into the room. He introduced himself as Dr. Fritsch. He had no trouble identifying Tim as the man he'd come to see. He told Tim he was a plastic surgeon. He wanted Tim to come with him to an examining room. Will followed explaining that Tim couldn't speak, they were buddies and he wanted to be with him.

In the examining room Fritsch said he'd reviewed Tim's case files. He wanted to know why this request hadn't been made much earlier. Will intervened. "Tim was pretty out of it for a long time after he got here. After that I guess he just thought this was it. This was the way he'd be from now on."

Dr. Fritsch looked skeptical. He examined Tim's face frowning all the while. He had Tim try to open and close his mouth while he felt the jaw with his fingers. He made lots of notes. Finally he said. "Okay, here's how I see it. I can graft some patches of skin into the cheeks on both sides of your face. That will relieve the tissue strain. That's the easy part. The tricky part is the injury to the facial muscles that lie just underneath the skin. We can try a new experimental procedure sewing extensions on to those muscles to lengthen them. I'll also snip a few of them to relax your face. That will allow you to close your mouth, and to chew. You're not able to do that now, are you?" Tim nodded. "The downside is, once that's done you'll only be able to show limited facial expression from your nose down." He gave as an example the act of smiling. Some of those muscles are responsible for drawing the cheeks and the mouth back," He demonstrated with his own face. "If you're a poker player, that could be an advantage. In other words, you'll have a poker face.

"Hell, Doc, he's already got a fixed expression, and it hurts him." Tim nodded his agreement. "Will he be able to talk?"

"When the surgeries, plural, are complete, you'll be almost entirely pain free. It remains to be seen how much the jaw muscles have atrophied from lack of use. Hopefully you'll get to where you'll be able to form most words and to chew, but it's not going to happen overnight. You'll need physical and massage therapy along with an exercise routine."

"When can we get started, and how long will it take?"

"I'll try to schedule him for the initial surgery later this week. It will take a few days before the bandages can be removed. We'll be able to do the second procedure in about a month to six weeks, barring infection. You'll be able to eat soft foods in small portions several times-a-day. If your jaw muscles will work you'll need to build their strength gradually. I wish this could have been done much earlier. The recovery process is going to take longer now."

Fritsch looked at both of them. "There's one other thing. I am going to need a skin donor for the grafts.

Will asked? "Can you use skin from me?"

Fritsch said he could. It would be taken off Will's thigh, and the recovery time for the skin to regenerate itself, would be the same for him as for Tim."

Will looked at Tim who gave a slight nod. "Okay, let's do it." Fritsch gave both of them some details about the first procedure. Before they left he told Tim he didn't know how he'd managed to endure being this way for so long. He'd do his best to help Tim get back to a more normal life.

On the way back to their room Tim wrote, "Thanks

Will."

Will replied. "I wasn't sure about him starting out, but he seems like a good guy. He seems to know what he's doing. I appreciate the time he took to explain what you're faced with.

Will explained to Leslie what was happening with Tim. He told her he'd volunteered to donate skin for the grafts. She understood the reason for the decisions he'd made. "I'm disappointed you're not going to be coming home right away, Will, but I think what you're doing is important for both of you. Besides, you need to get your stump healed so you can be fitted with a prosthesis."

Tim had his first surgeries on Friday. It combined two separate procedures. The first involved lengthening several facial muscles employing experimental micro-surgical techniques followed by extensive skin grafting. After ten hours in the operating room, Tim Sullivan was able to close his mouth and he no longer had a fixed mask-like grin. He was given a milk shake for supper and he was able to drink it using a straw. Tea got a big kick out of the fact that parts of Tim's face, neck and skull had skin from Will's legs. He told Tim if he'd known Tim needed some extra skin, he'd have given him some of his. "Wouldn't you be a sight with a face like that?"

Tim wrote, "Fuck you, Tea, I hope they give you a blue glass eye."

"A glass eye? I don't want no glass eye. Shit, man, I be wantin' a patch. I don't wants nothin' ta do with no glass fuckin' eye."

Leslie said, "Look at that pout. Hasn't Tea got one of the best pouts you've ever seen?"

Tea showed a slight smile, "Fuck you guys. You be pullin' my leg, aren't you?"

Chapter 16

Leslie had photographs with her that had been taken at the resort. She went through the stack with Tim and Tea, explaining most of them. "This is our dog Gabe. You and he have something in common, Tea. He lost an eye a few years back. That's a whole story by itself." There was a picture of Will and Feisty together. They were shirtless, wearing cut-offs, work boots and their tool belts. Tim recognized Frank immediately. He studied the picture and wrote, "He's grown a lot. I always thought he'd end up being short. We grew up together. His parents practically raised me." Tim wanted to know how he and Will had gotten to know one another. Will gave Tim a brief history of their relationship. Tim wanted to know if he'd get to see Noonan if he came to Wisconsin with them. They guaranteed it. Tim had several questions about Frank over the next few days.

That evening Leslie and Will went to the garden together. She helped him out of his wheel chair and she sat close to him on one of the benches. "I'm not sorry I nudged you to reach out to Tim. I'm glad you found a way to get through to him." She took his hand. "You need to see this through, Will." She admitted to feeling disappointed that his homecoming was going to be postponed probably for the entire summer. Will didn't come right out and say so, but he really wasn't feeling up to dealing with 'the summer crowd' and having to repeatedly explain how he'd lost his leg. The infection in his stump was healing but Will was frustrated with how long it was taking. The next step would be to fit him with a prosthesis. He anticipated it would take some getting used to, but he hoped it would make it easier for him to get around and he'd be able to resume a more normal life.

Leslie brought out a few other photographs she'd saved to share just with Will. There were two of Leslie with Merlin and two of Merlin by himself. She told Will the story of how she and Thomas had found the hawk. She talked about the significance Mary attached to them finding it, it's survival and it's specific injuries. Leslie went on to tell him about Norma Gray Eagle, and becoming Norma's apprentice. The last picture was of Will and Leslie taken from behind. They were stark naked and wading out into the lake with Gabe ahead of them. It looked like it was early in the morning. "Who took that picture?" Will asked.

"Feisty," Leslie told him. "Do you remember that morning, Will?" She slipped her arm across his shoulders."

"I do. It was our senior year in college. We went north to shut down the waterfront for the season. What a sneaky little shit."

"He gave me the picture to try to cheer me up." Will asked if it had. "No, mostly it made me horny, which made me even sadder." She hesitated, "Will, to tell you I've missed you doesn't come even close. I wish there was some place we could go to make love."

Will's response was somber. "Even if there was, I don't know if I can, Les. Something's wrong with me. I've thought back to the way things were between us sexually. Once we got started it was like we couldn't get enough of one another. I don't know what's going on with me. I don't know if it's something physical or if it's emotional." He told her about the condition he was in when he came to after being captured. "I don't know how long I'd been that way. I'm beginning to think it made me sterile." Leslie asked if he'd brought the subject up with any of his physicians. He told her he hadn't, "We've all been concerned about other things not my inability get it up. I guess I've just been hoping the problem would eventually go away on it's own." She asked if he even thought about sex. "I've thought about the way things used to be between us, but I don't find myself feeling horny. I never wake up with an erection. Christ, I don't even have fantasies anymore."

Leslie decided not to press the subject for fear of making things worse. She tried to hide her disappointment. "Will, today's Thursday. I've got to get back to the resort. We're heading into the busy time of the season. I'm going to leave on Saturday. It looks like Tim's surgeries are going to go on for most of the summer. When you two are ready to come home, I'll come get you."

"Les, I'm sorry. This isn't what either of us had hoped for."

"I know." She squeezed his hand and took a deep breath. "I think we're in for some big challenges, Will. We've been through a lot already." She studied him. He looked tired. His weight loss and the lines in his face made him look years older. "I just want you to know, I'll love you no matter what." He couldn't respond. She tried not to let her spirits sink any lower. She'd hoped their reunion would be joyous, and they'd be on their way home with Feisty and Sunny by now. She'd been counting on getting Will back to the lake thinking it would have a healing effect on him. Mary and Jeanne had told her not to expect him to open up to her about what had happened. If it came out it would be in fragments, like pieces of several puzzles, and without pictures to guide in their assembly. They'd both said basically the same thing about Will. Because of his sensitive nature he was going to go through a lot of turmoil in trying to recuperate emotionally. What they both knew and didn't say was there would be times when he'd think he couldn't make it.

They sat in silence for a while. Leslie finally said, "I'm amazed to discover Tim and Feisty practically grew up together."

"Yeah, me too. I'm surprised Feisty never mentioned anything about Tim." Will shifted the conversation. "I think Tim wants to come home with us but I think he's unsure. I get the feeling he thinks the invitation was all my idea. Maybe you can talk to him and let him know the offer comes from both of us." She agreed. She was worried about how Feisty was going to react to seeing his old friend this way. "I'd like to see pictures of Tim before he got burned. He's so disfigured, it's impossible to tell what he used to look like."

Leslie stopped by the unit early on Saturday morning to say goodbye to Will, Tim and Tea. Will went out to the cab stand with her. "I'm sorry, Will. I feel terrible about leaving. I wish I could afford to stay. I feel better about leaving knowing you and Tim will be there to help each other."

"Seeing Tim through these surgeries is important for both of us, Les. I'm feeling kind of lost right now. I don't know what I'm going to do with myself. I feel like being there for Tim gives me some purpose for the time being. I'm sure he wouldn't be doing any of this on his own. I don't know what's going to happen when I get back home. I've got a lot of figuring out to do. Christ, ninety percent of the guys here are a helluva lot worse off than me." They hugged and Will said, "Les, you've gotten even more beautiful, not just physically. I've missed you."

She became teary-eyed. "Thanks, Will. I really needed to hear that."

"One of the first places we'll go when I get home is the Dairy Queen."

Leslie gave a weak smile. "I know. That's where you

take all of the girls when they've had a rough day. I'm glad you still remember. It was the perfect solution."

When Will got back to the room, Tim was sitting on his bed applying ointment to his upper body. He stopped and looked at Will. He handed Will his note pad. He'd already written, 'You should have gone with her'.

Will sat down across from him. "I'm not here just for you, Tim. I'm here for me, too." He started to get up. Tim made a naaa sound. He gestured for Will to talk to him. "I don't know what to say." Tim's eyes remained fixed on him. "I'm fucked up." Tim wrote, 'We all are'. Then Tim changed direction and wrote. 'Leslie's beautiful. She loves you'. After several moments Will said, "I don't know if I can talk about this." Tim's eyes were steadfast. Will told him he knew Leslie loved him. He loved her, too." In capital letters Tim wrote, 'BUT'. Will took a deep breath and explained the problem he was having with impotency. He repeated the things he'd said to Leslie about his lack of sexual interest. When Will finished, Tim wrote, 'Let's go to the garden'. Tea was sound asleep. Tim helped Will into his wheelchair.

Will asked if Tim had a girlfriend. He shook his head. "How about sex. You're not a virgin, are you?" Tim shook his head again. "That's a relief." Tim wrote that he'd really liked one of Noonan's sisters. They'd done it a few times. Will asked what happened with that relationship. Tim wrote, 'They moved. Never saw her again'. Will asked which sister, Feisty had three. Tim wrote, 'The oldest, Claire'. "Good choice, Tim. She was a real vixen."

Tim began seeing a speech pathologist on a daily basis learning how to enunciate. The fact that he could make sounds indicated his vocal chords hadn't atrophied, or been scorched, but he was going to require prolonged speech therapy. In the beginning he spoke slowly and deliberately sounding almost robotic. He was self conscious about it and most of what he said was reserved to conversations with Will and a few of the staff.

Tim's second surgery was three weeks later. This one involved removing the ropey keloided scar tissue that had formed on his back, shoulders, chest and arms. It required some additional grafting. The skin used came from a recently deceased patient. For the next several days after the surgery Tim had to be monitored constantly both to manage the pain and for any signs of infection. As it was explained to both of them, it was tantamount to him being burned all over again, but without anything like the agony he'd gone through before. The good news was, once he was healed, he'd have full mobility, range of motion and significantly less pain.

Tim was kept in isolation for over two weeks following the surgery in order to minimize the chances of infection. One of the nurses consoled Will by saying, "Tim's on so much pain medication right now, you two wouldn't be able to carry on a conversation anyhow."

The infection in Will's stump continued to improve and it was less painful. Until it healed completely he couldn't be fitted with a prosthesis. He tried to avoid using his wheel chair opting for his crutches as much as possible. He pushed himself trying to develop strength and stamina. When he over-did it, he paid a price, suffering pain in his right shoulder and upper back. At times he wondered if the Hmong medicine man were here, would he be of more help than the Army doctors.

Tea left the hospital the day after Tim was allowed to return to their room. Will expressed his doubt they'd ever see him again. He told Tim the story of his one-eyed dog Gabe, and how that had come to be. He wasn't thinking when he told Tim about the bears coming into the resort. It aroused all sorts of concerns. Tim wasn't so sure he wanted to live in a place like that.

Leslie called twice a week. Tim would leave the room to give Will some privacy. Leslie was keeping notes about what was going on at the resort. Will had come to know the majority of the regular guests and she was sure he'd like hearing about them. The daily routine of the hospital didn't provide him with much to share. Will had learned wood carving from one of the guests his first summer at the resort twelve years ago. He'd continued on with it and developed into a fairly skilled carver. He decided to talk to Cathy, the OT, to see if she had someplace he could do some wood carving. She invited him to come down to their workshop and she even offered to see about getting him some tools. "I've got tools and blanks at home. Leslie can send them to me. I just need a place to work." She took both of them to the rehab building and showed them the large craft workshop. There were a number of patients at various stations working on craft projects. There was a sign on Cathy's office door that read, 'Busy hands do a happy person make'. Will asked if he could come to the workshop on a daily basis.

A week later his tools along with two-dozen blanks arrived. A note from Thomas promised him additional blanks if he'd send patterns. Will had used the wait-time to draw up a number of them. He and Tim went to the workshop three mornings a week from then on. Before long Will had five other patients taking carving lessons. Cathy ordered tools and band-aids. Tim sat nearby painting.

Tim was holding an umbrella over the two of them one rainy morning on their way back to the 'ward' as they'd come to call it. Tim's speech was getting better. Words with 'R' sounds remained difficult for him. He could say happy, but happier was close to impossible.

Will brought up the Hmong people he'd lived with again. "Words with 'L's and 'R's were impossible for them. I don't think those sounds were a part of their language. I gave up on trying to teach them to say my name."

"So, what did they call you?"

"Gimpy."

"You be shitting me?" Will smiled at him. "You seem much happy now, Will."

"You do too, Tim."

Tim asked how he'd kept from going crazy while he was a prisoner. "I don't remember any of it. I don't know how long they'd held me before they abandoned me." He told Tim some of the details of his condition when he became conscious. Tim was amazed he'd managed to survive. They both thought that of one another. It would be a long time before they were able to bring themselves to talk about having wanted to die.

By early August, Will's stump was considered healed and he was fitted with a prosthesis. He received his new leg the last week in August and he began working with a physical therapist learning how to walk with it. Despite being warned not to push himself too hard, he did, wearing off a patch of the tender skin on his stump. He was almost back to square one having to wait until the skin healed before he could resume using it.

Chapter 17

Both Tim and Will were told they could be released from the hospital after Labor Day. Leslie, Feisty and Sunny decided to wait until after the holiday weekend to drive to D.C.

They left for the hospital on Wednesday and drove straight through taking turns sleeping in the back of Jeanne's minivan. When they came into the room, Feisty and Will hugged one another. "Christ Will, you've lost a lot of weight. Haven't they been feeding you or is the food here that terrible?"

Will turned to, Tim. "Feisty do you remember this guy?"

Tim said, "Frankie, long time no see."

Feisty squinted at him. "Rusty? Is that you?" Tim nodded. "Can I hug you?" Feisty hugged him cautiously. He told everyone Tim used to have curly, flamin' red hair, and lot's of it."

Tim reached for his toupee on the table next to his bed and slipped it on. Leslie adjusted it

"Nope," Feisty shook his head. "Rusty's hair wasn't that bright, and it was real curly, and longer. This is bullshit. We're gonna get you a wig that looks more like the way you used to." Will could see the delight in Tim's eyes. He wished Tim could show more of a smile. Will would need to explain Tim's lack of expression to them later. After hugging Tim, Leslie commented on the changes in him. She knew from what Will had said, Tim was able to talk now, but she hadn't expected his voice to sound so mechanical and mono-tonal. She wondered if that would improve over time.

Addressing Tim, Feisty, asked, "I don't suppose you're able to play guitar anymore?" Tim shook his head. Feisty turned to the others. "Rusty here was one of the best guitarists in the city." He turned back to Tim. "Man, We've got to find some way of getting' you back to playin'. We'll figure somethin' out. Maybe we can get you a Dobro so you won't have to finger the strings. Leslie asked what a Dobro was. "It's a different kind of guitar. It's also called a resonator. It's got a metal body that looks kinda like a pasta strainer. Some of the old time black blues guitarists played them." He explained how the guitar was tuned to whatever key the guitarist chose. Instead of having to press the strings down using the finger tips, the guitarist used a slide bar. "Rusty and I used to sneak into some of blues bars after they closed for the night. Sometimes the musicians would let us honkies sit in with them. We regarded it as an honor. Rusty was so good he was able to teach them some new riffs they hadn't heard before." Leslie asked what the term 'honkies' meant. "White guys."

Will and Tim were checked out of the hospital early the next morning. Will's stump was still very tender. His physician gave him a different antibiotic to take along in case it began to flare up again. Tim still needed light bandaging where they'd removed the scar tissue.

Feisty had hoped they'd have the time to make a leisurely scenic trip back home. He and Sunny were still living in Chicago. He'd finished his architectural internship and had been hired by the same firm where he'd done his practicum. Sunny had switched hospitals and was now working at Children's Memorial Hospital on the northside. Neither of them could afford to be away from their jobs for more than a week. It meant they needed to make a fairly quick turn-around trip. Leslie had driven down to the city using Jeanne's minivan. She picked them up for the marathon journey to

Washington.

Will was worried he might not be able to drive ever again. He knew he'd never be able to use his jeep. He might be able to have an automatic transmission installed in his old truck. Otherwise he'd have to buy a newer one. He gave some thought to asking Leslie to give Tim her car, and they'd buy her a minivan.

Feisty, Sunny and Leslie took turns driving, switching off every couple of hours. None of them were pushing it and they engaged in continuous conversations. Tim was reluctant about talking at first, but he eventually joined in. He had questions about what it was like living in 'the Great Northwoods'. He pictured it as being remote and uncivilized. He was worried about the winters knowing he was cold-sensitive. It was Feisty, in his unabashed direct way, who addressed Tim's greatest fear and concern by asking, "Tim, I get the feelin' you're worried about how you look. You think people are going to see you as bein' some kinda freak."

Tim came right back at him, "Well, yeah. Fuckin' look at me. That's what I am."

Feisty's retort was. "That's how you see yourself, Tim. I'll admit you don't look like the same dude I used to know. Your appearance takes a little getting' used to. But, you're still the same gentle, talented guy beneath the exterior. There's gonna be some people who are gonna get hung up on how you look. Screw em, they'll never know what they're missin'."

Will was watching Tim. He sensed Tim was feeling skeptical and not in agreement with what Feisty had just said. Will reached over and touched Tim's shoulder and nodded toward Feisty. "I've never known him to tell people what they want to hear. Nor is he particularly diplomatic." Tim nodded then made an effort to show a slight smile.

They stopped early that evening in a town north east

of Toledo. Feisty had heard it was wine country and there were supposed to be some excellent wineries in the area. After finding a motel they visited a couple of them and ended up buying three cases of wine. One of them was for Jeanne. They somehow managed to pack them into the already stuffed van. The town itself was picturesque with a stream that ran right through the center of its downtown area. They found a restaurant located next to the brook. The evening was so pleasant the five of them opted to sit outside on a patio.

Tim was quiet throughout dinner. He didn't seem down about anything. Mostly he listened to the others talking. Will asked, "How are you doing? You haven't said much."

"I'm fine, Will. It's just that I've never seen people enjoy one another as much as the four of you do. I'm in awe. You guys really do like one another. How long has it been since you've seen one another?"

"Over two years."

"What amazes me the most is you act like you just saw one another yesterday. You just jumped in like you've never been apart. Will told Tim he couldn't bring himself to call him Rusty. "I'd prefer you call me Tim. Rusty's gone. I got that nickname because of my red hair. I'm going to ask Frank to call me Tim." That got Will to thinking that maybe the name he'd given Frank Noonan years before was a thing of the past, too.

They had breakfast at a small Mom and Pop restaurant before hitting the road. It reminded Leslie, Will and Feisty of Angelo's diner, a place they'd congregated at back in their junior high days. They arrived at Feisty and Sunny's place just ahead of the Chicago evening rush hour traffic. The sky looked ominous to the west. Will predicted they were in for some thunderstorms.

Frank asked Tim if he wanted to go back to see the old neighborhood tomorrow. Tim shrugged. "I joined the Army to get away from there, Frank. After you moved away I started getting into trouble. I got busted a few times. Your old man stepped in to bail me out on two or three occasions. He even offered me a place to stay. I have no reason to go back there. The only good thing about it for me was the music. That's over with. I'm not going to be able to play again."

Feisty talked about his father nearing retirement. "I can't see Dominic retired. He'll go freakin' stir crazy. Ma's going to go nuts havin' him around all the time."

Will made a suggestion. "You ought to talk to your dad about buying a bar up north. He'd like doing something like that. I know of one that also sells fishing tackle and bait. Your dad loves fishing. He'd be happy as hell."

"He would, but Ma wouldn't. She's got family she's close to. Family's everything to her." Feisty's wheels were turning. "I really like the idea though." Feisty asked Sunny what she thought.

"I like the idea, too, but I don't think it will ever happen. Dominic would like being there during the summer when it's crowded and busy. What would he do with himself the other seven months of the year?"

The five of them sat around in the small apartment drinking beer and talking that evening. Sunny was particularly interested in the surgeries Tim had gone through over the past three months. She asked if he was going to require any more. Tim found it difficult to talk about the way he'd been before. He didn't mind talking about the procedures he'd undergone over the summer. He appreciated that Dr. Fritsch had taken the time to explain what he was going to do each step of the way. He regarded himself as both 'a work in progress' and an experimental guinea pig. The extensions to his facial muscles were an experimental procedure made possible because of advances in micro-surgical techniques. He hoped other innovations would come along in the near future to help restore him even closer to 'normal'.

Sunny picked up on what he'd just said. She thought 'closer to normal' was a good way to look at it. She complimented him for his realistic outlook."

They were all up early the next morning. Leslie, Will and Tim wanted to avoid as much rush-hour traffic as possible. Sunny and Frank had to be at work by eight.

It surprised Will there was so much outbound traffic leaving the city. He hadn't realized that an enormous shift had taken place as large businesses moved out to the suburbs. He wanted to hear Frank's take on this reverse trend.

Until Tim joined the Army, he'd never been out to Chicago. He'd seldom been out of the southside. As they neared the I-90 bridge that crossed the Fox river, Will asked Leslie to slow down so he could point the river out to Tim. He spent the next hour telling Tim about the adventures he and Leslie and Frank had shared living close to the river during their teen years. The one that captured Tim's attention the most was about the old hermit, Emil Bergstrom, who lived in a shack right on the river. "I thought when it came time for me to leave the hospital I'd go south, somewhere warm. I'd try to find a small place out in the woods where I didn't have to be around people. Even though I look better now, I'm still self-conscious about my appearance and the way I talk."

Will said, "Tim you're a city guy. How would you get by living out in the woods somewhere?"

"I'd find a way. If I didn't, it really wouldn't matter."

"It would matter to us, Tim." Leslie said. She surprised Will when she then said. "You're not a freak, Tim. Don't get yourself all hung up on looks. You've got a great personality, and you're a nice person." Tim thanked her and fell into silence.

They arrived at the resort a little after four. Augie

and Thomas were working to put together a second dock. They were about done for the day. Gabe alerted Jeanne of their arrival with his bark. Both dogs ran to greet them. Will got out of the van and managed to kneel as the dogs wagged and licked and pranced around in excitement. He hugged them. "Look at the two of you. You've got gray hair on your faces. You old dogs, you." Jeanne came from the house and hugged them. Leslie handed Will his crutches and they started down the hill toward the lake.

Augie and Thomas dropped what they were doing and came toward them. Will embraced Thomas. They held one another for several moments. "It's good to have you home, Will." They studied one another. Thomas looked the same except for having grayed considerably letting his hair grow. He wore it in a pony tail. Will introduced him to Tim. He'd already told Tim about Thomas and Mary.

Augie greeted Tim warmly. "Will told me about the string of surgeries you just finished, Tim. How come it took them so long to get around to doing them?" Tim explained it was his fault. He'd been through so much, he'd just given up. He changed the subject. "What a beautiful place you have, Augie. The Lake is nicer than I'd imagined."

Will asked Augie what he and Thomas were up to. Augie motioned for them to come see for themselves. Thomas said he needed to take off for home. He'd see them tomorrow. As they began walking out on the new dock, Augie put a hand on Tim's shoulder. "Feisty, tells me the two of you grew up together in Chicago. This must seem pretty foreign to you." Augie chuckled, "It sure was for him the first time he came here." Gabe ran out ahead of them and at the end at of the dock he dove in. Sally stayed close to Will.

"Gabe thinks it's swim time and he's expecting all of

us to join him," Augie showed them what he and Thomas were in the process of doing. "We've decided to add a large square floating extension. "We need space to dock boats, but we also thought this could be an area for swimming and sun bathing during the day, and enjoying sunsets in the evening."

Tim looked down in the water, "Wow, look at all the fish! And look, you can even see the bottom." He looked at Frank, "I've never been fishing? Can we go sometime?"

"Sure. We can go out for a while this evening if you feel like it."

"Can you swim in the lake, too," Tim asked?

"We do it practically every day, and the water's perfect this time of the year. It's had all summer to warm up." Augie asked if Tim had ever been lake swimming.

"Me? I've never been swimming in my life."

"We'll teach you." Augie said. There's nothing nicer than skinny dipping on a warm summer's evening. Well, almost nothing." Will and Frank glanced at one another. Tim didn't know it yet, but Augie was adopting another son. Tim was now a part of the family.

Chapter 18

Frank drove them to Will and Leslie's cabin. Will had named it August Loon years before. It was only a short distance away and they piled into Feisty's surplus Army jeep circa the early 1950's, Korean War vintage. Will had one just like it. Tim was shown his room. He only had one change of clothes. Leslie and Will offered to take him into town in the morning to open a bank account, and to do some shopping. He wasn't sure what kind of clothes to buy. He explained that before joining the Army all of his clothes had come from resale shops. "I bought what fit. I looked pretty funky most of time."

Feisty said, "Naw, Man. You looked hip. You fit right in with most of the south-side musicians. However, living up here, you'd stand out like a unicorn."

Frank invited Will and Tim to hike the short distance to where he and Sunny were putting up their house. He'd designed it and the two of them were doing most of the work themselves. It was on property Augie had inherited that was between the resort and the August Loon cabin. Augie had set up a trust so that he and Jeanne retained ownership of all of the land along the lake shore to the east side of August Loon. The parcel Will and Leslie had, and the one Feisty and Sunny were building on would become theirs when Augie and Jeanne were gone.

On the way Feisty explained he planned to move up here in the next couple of years and start his own firm. Sunny had applications in for a nursing job at the local hospital/clinic in town. It didn't matter to her that she was earning three times more working in the city. She'd lived here most of her life, and she wanted to return to her home-place.

Will was impressed with the design and doubly impressed they'd managed to accomplish this much working part-time and mostly by themselves. Tim knew nothing about construction, but he was amazed that Frank and Sunny had taken on such a big project. "I never figured you for being one to work with your hands, Frank. I guess I saw you becoming a cop like your old man."

When they returned to the cabin Norma Gray Eagle was there. She had Merlin with her. Leslie had told Will a lot about her. She wasn't quite what he'd expected. She was tall and muscular. Her long gray hair hung in a loose braid past the middle of her back. Will thought she could be an attractive woman if it weren't for her missing some teeth. Her jeans were faded and threadbare. She wore a lightweight flannel shirt with the sleeves rolled up revealing sinewy muscular arms. Her face was weathered making her look older than she probably was. He recalled Leslie telling him Norma was the same age as Augie.

Will glanced over at her beat up, rusty old pickup truck, wondering what kept it running. He imagined the under-body was so full of holes it must be like a sieve. *She must freeze in that thing during the winter.*

He realized Norma was studying him as they approached. He wondered how much she knew about what had happened to him. *Probably quite a bit, since she was brought in at the beginning when Thomas and Leslie rescued the bird.* Leslie had Merlin and was about to tether him to a stump out in the yard. Norma walked toward Will and extended her hand. Then she turned to shake hands with Tim. She held onto his hand and asked if most of his burns were upper body. He told her the backs of his legs had been badly burned, too. "Both of you have been through a lot. This is a good place to mend yourselves."

She turned and nodded in Leslie's direction. "That's Merlin. I'm sure Leslie's told you how he helped us to keep track of you, Will. It was pretty touch and go for the first few weeks.

Will asked, "Did you think if you were able to keep him alive, it would somehow save me?"

"I don't know, Will. That's what Mary and the others thought. I tended to be more skeptical. I don't buy into much of that Indian hocus-pocus about spiritual connections." She was sensitive to Will's lack of response. "I know that sounds critical. I'm glad both you and Tim made it back. The way I look at it is, you wouldn't have if you weren't determined to make it and you'd given up." Norma turned and called to Leslie, telling her to let Merlin fly.

Leslie took off his hood and tether. He stepped on to her gauntlet and she launched him. Merlin flew toward the lake flapping his wings no more than five or six times. He found an updraft and began to ascend. He circled back, flapped his wings a few more times finding another, and another. He kept climbing and in a short time he was high up soaring out over the lake. He gave an almost joyous screech of freedom. Leslie walked toward the group.

"What's to keep him from flying away?" Tim asked.

"The relationship" Norma said, shielding her eyes from the sun so she could keep track of him. She explained, "Leslie and Merlin have formed a special bond. Merlin's become imprinted on her, meaning he recognizes her as his caregiver." She watched the bird making lazy circles over the lake. "Isn't that a magnificent sight?" Still focused on the hawk, Norma said, "It remains to be seen whether he'll leave here to migrate."

She turned her attention to Will. "One of the amazing things about what happened is that Leslie and Thomas found him two days before Christmas. You were captured on Christmas Eve day. Vietnam is a day ahead of us. He was caught in a trap. There was close to three feet of snow on the ground, and frigid temperatures. I've never seen a hawk here in the winter. Leslie's told you the story about finding him, hasn't she?"

Will nodded. He was intent on watching the hawk himself. "Tim hasn't heard it. I'll let Leslie tell him the story." Leslie called to Will and waved for him to come over to where she stood close to the stump. Norma accompanied him saying, "Leslie's a natural at handling injured critters. It isn't just Merlin."

Leslie had Will put on the gauntlet. She touched his back, "Hold your arm out, Will." Then she gave a loud whistle. Merlin was circling out over the lake. He suddenly began a rapid descent. "Don't worry, he'll brake his fall at the last second. You'll be amazed." Seconds later, with his wings held out rigidly and his tail feathers fanned, the hawk landed on Will's arm as if he'd stepped onto the glove. Will was amazed at how he'd managed to land so effortlessly and how little he weighed.

"Jesus, that was incredible," Will exclaimed.

"Isn't it? Leslie said as she stroked Merlin's head and spoke to the bird in soothing tones. "That was a perfect landing, Merlin." She gave Merlin a piece of raw chicken, telling Will. "He gets a reward for a job well done." She coaxed Merlin onto the stump and tethered him before putting on his leather hood. "Norma, can you hang around for dinner? We're going to enjoy some wine and the sunset at Augie and Jeanne's. Augie's cooking out."

Norma was reluctant. "I suppose. The creatures will be okay, but I can't stay very late."

Leslie put Merlin in his cage and removed his hood. Tim asked if that was to keep him from flying away. "It's mostly to protect him from other predators that might come along." Leslie said. "I don't think he'll fly away, not now. Hopefully he'll join other hawks during the fall migration."

"You really like doing the animal rehab work don't you?" Will asked.

"I love it, I can hardly wait for you to come out to Norma's place to see what we're doing. I've learned so much in the short time I've spent working with her. I think she knows more than a lot of veterinarians. She relies on vets mostly for medication. The one she gets along with and trusts the most is Doug Kenyon." Will remembered Doug. He'd treated Gabe when the dog was injured by a bear a few years earlier.

At the resort, Augie asked Will if he wanted to join him in having a martini. Everyone was gathered out on the deck. Tim asked Augie several questions about the resort. Augie explained how his parents had immigrated to this country from Norway and homesteaded this place in the early 1900's."I'll show you a map of the area later."

Leslie came over to Will and touched his back, "How are you doing, you look really tired?"

"I'm okay. I just need to sit down." He eased himself into a deck chair.

She pulled a chair up next to him. "You're in a lot of pain, aren't you?" He took a swallow of the martini and told her his stump was hurting. "Since when did you start drinking hard liquor?"

He looked at his glass then at her. "Les, I hate to be a party-pooper, but I need to go lie down. Can you take me back to the cabin? I'm beat all to hell." She nodded and went to ask Frank if they'd bring Tim home. She told Jeanne and Tim that Will was in a lot of pain. She was taking him back to the cabin.

Norma had been watching what was going on. She stooped down in front of Will. "What's going on, Will? You look like you're running a fever. You're sweating." She leaned forward and felt his forehead.

"I'm feeling kind of dizzy, I need to go lay down."

Tim came over. Will was just starting to shiver. Tim set his beer down and used his thumbs to lower Will's eyelids. "Have you had malaria, Will?" Will shook his head. He didn't think so. "If you did, you'd know it." Norma asked if Tim thought that was what was wrong with him. Leslie was telling Augie she was going to take Will back to their cabin. Augie asked Frank to watch the grill and he came over. Will's shivering was becoming pronounced. Tim asked where the nearest hospital was. "I think Will's got malaria."

"Christ, I doubt our doctors have ever seen a case of malaria. Let's get him in my car."

Norma asked Tim what they should do. "See if Jeanne's got some light weight blankets. His shivering is going to get worse. He's already sweating." He asked Jeanne if they had any tonic water. "It's got quinine in it. That will help."

Augie pulled his car up close to the house. He and Frank half carried Will and put him in the back seat. Frank volunteered to sit next to him to hang on to him in case Will became convulsive. Tim rode up front. Leslie put the dogs in the house while Jeanne and Sunny hurriedly put things away. Norma apologized for not being able to accompany them; she needed to head for home to tend to her critters. She asked Leslie to call her later. On the way to the hospital Leslie turned to Sunny. "This is crazy. Will's been out of Vietnam for over five months. Why is he showing symptoms now? What's the incubation period? What the hell is malaria anyhow?" Sunny admitted she didn't know much about it other than it was a mosquito-born parasite that attacked the liver and kidneys. She didn't know how it was treated or if there were any real cures for it. People with malaria often had recurring bouts of the symptoms for years. Jeanne asked if it could be deadly. Sunny tried to downplay the likelihood Will was in jeopardy. "Is there a chance he could have gotten it while he was at Reed hospital?" Sunny doubted it.

By the time the ladies arrived at the hospital Will had been admitted. It turned out the ER doctor had spent a year working at a hospital in the Panama Canal Zone and he'd seen a number of Malaria patients. He'd already done a blood smear, which confirmed the diagnosis. The bad news was, the medications needed to fight the infection weren't available. It would take a day to get them. The Doc was forthright in telling them Will was in for a miserable next twenty-four hours. Tim was visibly worried. Frank tried to console him by complimenting him for seeing something was wrong and being able to identify it. "Jesus, Tim. What if Leslie had taken him home? Who knows what would have happened? Things would have just gotten worse for him."

Tim shook his head, "My old man was with the Marines in the Pacific. He got malaria. I saw what he went through when it flared up. It was the only time he was ever sober. He was too fucking sick to drink. It made him so weak he could barely get out of bed to make it to the toilet. He'd be like that for a couple of weeks." Augie asked Tim if his father was still alive. Tim had no idea. He hadn't seen him since leaving home at sixteen.

Leslie picked up on Tim's biggest concern. He was worried about what would happen if Will didn't survive. She expressed her concern to Frank. She was worried that if Will didn't survive Tim would leave. In his usual proactive style, Frank said he'd talk to Tim himself. "He needs to know he's got a place here no matter what."

The ER doctor met with them to explain Will's condition and to answer their questions. The big one was how serious a threat was this to Will's survival. He admitted Will was in jeopardy. "Will's not in the best condition because of the infection he's been fighting with his leg. I was able to talk to one of the infectious disease docs at Reed. He gave me some suggestions for some additional approaches we can take. Our local pharmacist is in the process of formulating an intravenous cocktail. It should help to reduce most of his symptoms."

After the meeting with the ER doctor they all decided there wasn't any point to sticking around the hospital. Frank and Sunny were staying at their place so they left with Leslie and Tim. On the way Sunny asked if Leslie was going to go back to the hospital. "I haven't decided. I'm wiped out from the trip home, and now this. It's going to be a long night." Nobody but Frank wanted anything to drink. He had a beer and Leslie poured iced tea for the rest of them. They went out to sit on the front porch and Gabe curled up next to Tim.

After a period of silence Frank said to Tim, "You're not thinkin' of leavin', are you?"

When he didn't answer, Leslie said, "You're not in the way, Tim. Will's going to make it through this. He'll be devastated if you're not here when he comes home. It's like what Frank said. If it weren't for you, I'd have brought Will home and he wouldn't be getting the help he needs."

Leslie realized she'd forgotten all about Merlin. There was just enough daylight left she could release him for a brief while. Tim accompanied her and watched as she took the hawk from his cage, and prepared to let him fly. Before releasing him she scratched his head. It seemed incongruous watching this fierce looking raptor acting like a pet. She almost tossed him skyward and he took off. Watching him gain altitude she said, "This time of the day there aren't a lot of convection currents that provide updrafts. Hawks are great at finding thermals and soaring, but they're not real strong fliers. Even out over the lake he had to work at staying aloft. He finally came back on his own, landing perfectly on the stump. Leslie had a pouch with pieces of chicken. She fed him before returning him to the cage.

Norma called a while later to ask about Will. She wondered if malaria could be transmitted to animals and birds by mosquitoes, too. She commented about Tim. "I can't imagine what he's been through. He's got a gentle spirit. He's like an injured bird. He's afraid of being hurt by others. It says a lot that you and Will have been able to earn his trust."

"I think he'd almost given up hope. It was serendipity that we happened to come along when we did. I don't think he would have stuck around much longer."

Leslie had just hung up with Norma when Tim came in the house and said he was going to bed. They hugged one another unsure of what to say. Her fear was that Will had managed to survive all these other things, and now was in jeopardy of being brought down by a stupid micro-organism. The phone rang again. It was Thomas. Tim waved to her as he headed for the bathroom. Leslie said, "I suppose you already know what's going on with Will."

"Mary knows he's sick and that it's serious, but she hasn't seen this kind of sickness before." Leslie told him Will had malaria, sharing the little she knew about the disease. "From what I've heard that's nasty stuff. Will's been through so much already. He didn't need this." He paused. "We're glad you brought Tim home with you. The two of them have a lot of healing to do. They need each other." Leslie agreed. Thomas hesitated before saying, "We know this wasn't the homecoming you'd hoped for, Leslie." She wanted to say, 'You have no idea, Thomas'. She'd never experienced such terrible disappointment in her life A voice inside her was screaming, *What about me? I've got needs, too. I just want my husband back.* Before hanging up Thomas told Leslie they were there for all three of them. He added, "Most people don't realize the war goes on long after the troops come home. Looking back, Augie's parents must have felt terribly sad and helpless watching the two of us struggle with our demons." After hanging up Leslie poured a glass of wine. She and Gabe went out to sit on the porch.

Chapter 19

Will responded fairly quickly to the anti-malarial drugs and was able to return home after five days. He was told he'd need to stay on the medications for at least another two weeks to ensure against a relapse and they'd need to monitor his blood twice-a-week. He was also advised to abstain from imbibing alcohol. That wasn't difficult the first few days. He was still feeling crummy, not the words he used to describe the way he felt. He lacked energy, or interest in doing much of anything. Little things annoyed him. He tried not to take his frustration out on others. He'd either suppress his irritation or mumble something cynical under his breath. Whenever something wasn't going right he'd say 'screw it', not the word he employed, and he'd give up and walk away. Other times he'd berate himself saying such things as, 'brilliant Morrissey', 'you're dumber than a box of rocks', 'you'd screw up a manure pile', etcetera. Leslie was worried about his mental state. In a conversation with Jeanne she expressed her concern. "I thought Will would be glad to be back home. Instead, he's depressed as hell. I'm afraid to say anything for fear of how he'll react. I feel like I'm living with a time bomb. I hate to say it. Will's always said he never wanted to end up being like his father, but he's starting to behave that way."

Jeanne told her she'd felt that same way when she'd been in the throes of her cancer therapy. "It brought out the worst in me. I don't know how Augie was able to put up with my moodiness and sarcasm." She suggested Leslie go see Mary. She told her about the things Mary had gone through with Thomas after he and Augie had come home from Korea. "I didn't meet Augie until a few years later. His mother told me he was terribly restless when he came home. He'd always been an outgoing people-person, the way he is now. He was almost the opposite when he returned. He didn't want anything to do with the resort or dealing with the guests. He acted like he couldn't stand to live here anymore. He left even before the season was over and went to live in Chicago. He went from job to job and girl-friend to girl-friend. His mother had no idea how he ended up getting into selling insurance or starting his own agency. They rarely saw him. He seldom called and he never wrote. She said that went on for over five years. Then one day, out of the blue, he called and asked if he could come up for a visit. It was just a few days before Thanksgiving. She and Pops had pretty much decided the next season was going to be their last one. Even though they were still healthy, running the resort was getting to be too much for them. They planned to sell this place. Augie arrived and stayed until that Sunday. While he was here they told him of their plans to sell. A couple of days after he returned to Illinois he called and asked if he could buy the place from them. He told them they could stay on for as long as they wanted. He came up the following week-end and they discussed the terms." Leslie asked Jeanne if Augie had ever revealed anything about what had been going on with him during that period of time. Did she think it was tied to what happened to him in Korea?

Jeanne looked like she was debating what to say or even if she should go any further. "I didn't find out about Augie's hiatus from here until a few years later. I guess it was one of those family secrets. His mother was the one who told me. I asked the same question. Did she think it had something to do with his war experiences? She thought that was a large part of it. She said both Augie and Thomas came back changed men. They'd grown up together and had always been close friends. After they returned they seldom saw one another. She thought a part of it for Augie was that he felt stuck here. He wanted more out of life than struggling just to make ends meet. I later found out how little income the resort actually generated. His parents managed to eke out a living only because they lived so frugally. If Augie had stayed he'd have needed to find work during the off-season. You know how scarce good paying jobs are around here.

Leslie commented that Augie seemed to have resolved the past. He seemed content with life now. Jeanne showed an 'if you only knew smile'. "Augie's insurance agency has done well in large part because he's pretty hyper and ambitious. Some would even say he's driven. He's always got several things going on at once. A few years back, the summer Will came to stay with us, he decided to put up a new cabin. It was an experiment. He wanted to see what it would involve, and if it would be financially feasible. What I didn't realize was, for years, he'd been secretly entertaining fantasies of transforming this place. I'm convinced Augie's method of coping with his war experiences has been to pour himself into work." Jeanne paused briefly. "Augie and I love one another, but neither of us could tolerate being stranded on a desert isle together. One of the ways we've been able to sustain our marriage is by my being here and him being in Illinois and him coming for weekend visits. It's been a real challenge for both of us since he sold his business and moved up here. About the only good thing to have come out of my having cancer is that he's settled down quite a bit. I don't know if we'd still be together otherwise.

Leslie shook her head. She told Jeanne she was surprised by the things she was hearing. She'd seen the two of them as having an almost idyllic relationship. "I'm scared Jeanne. Will and I have been best friends for years. We've enjoyed each others company and doing things together. We became a real team during the months you were going through the cancer treatments. I feel like he's lost, like he doesn't know which way to turn. I guess I had some starry-eyed notion that getting him back here was going to make everything better. I'm beginning to realize it's going to be mostly up to him to find his way back and to find himself. I miss him and I want him back. I don't want to go through the rest of my life like my mother, having a part-time relationship with my husband." Jeanne refrained from saying, 'thirty or forty percent of something is better than one-hundred percent of nothing'. She realized she had no basis for judging Leslie's relationship with Will. Her relationship with Augie was the reverse of theirs. She'd been the damaged one, having come from an extremely abusive dysfunctional family, and a destructive marriage. Augie had worked hard to get her to open up and allow herself to trust him. He'd been good for her. He'd done a lot to coax her out of her fortress.

"That's why I think you need to go talk to Mary. She went through hell with Thomas for two or three years after he returned. She almost lost him." Jeanne switched to talking about herself and Augie. "I've never known what to believe about my relationship with Augie. Over the years I've seen him go through periods of moodiness where he withdraws and he barely talks to me. When that happens my insecurities kick in and I think he wants out of the relationship. It's taken me a long time to realize it has very little to do with me or our relationship. There have been times when he's had to force himself to go to the office and try to go through the motions of conducting business." Jeanne stopped herself. She apologized saying she realized she was sounding pretty gloomy about what lay ahead. "We've seen Will go through some amazing changes over the years, Leslie. I'm sure you have, too. We have a lot of faith in him. I don't know Tim, but I think the two of them are survivors. I'm glad you decided to bring him here. I think the two of them are going to find ways to help one another to build new lives."

Later that day Jeanne found herself reflecting on their conversation. She thought back to the three weeks in August Will had spent with them several years ago. Maybe it was because of the terrible way Will's father had treated him during the week the Morrissey family stayed at the resort. It had reopened some of her old wounds. She'd found herself sharing things about her own past with that fourteen year old boy, she'd never told anyone before, not even Augie. She thought her revelations to Will were an effort to let him know she understood what he was going through. What she hadn't realized at the time, was, in so doing, she'd had to reexamine how the abuses she'd suffered had affected her own life. It turned out to have a cathartic effect helping her to let go of many of her crippling fears. As a result she found herself feeling better about herself. She was able to open herself up, becoming more alive and creative and able to give and receive love.

She thought about Will. *No one knows what happened to him after he was captured. I doubt he's told anyone about what he endured. If he's confided in anyone, it's probably Tim. Maybe they've been able to share some of what's happened to each of them with one another. If so, that would help explain why Will invited Tim to come home with him. They need one another. They've both been through unspeakable hells and they're both struggling to make new lives for themselves and put those experiences behind them. They've formed an alliance sensing neither of them has the strength to survive on their own, at least not for now.*

Jeanne knew Leslie was desperate and searching for a way to help Will recover. She remembered some things Mama Nelson had said to her years before. She'd told Jeanne how Augie was before he'd gone to Korea and how he was when he came back. She described both Thomas and him as 'changed men'. Neither of them were relaxed and carefree anymore. They both seemed to take everything too seriously. 'When Augie announced his decision to leave for the city, neither of us tried to talk him out of it. Pa took the attitude Augie was lost and he needed to find himself. Having him gone was better than having him here feeling so miserable'.

Jeanne thought about the Augie she knew. He'd managed to 'find himself' prior to their meeting one another. He wasn't the sullen, malcontent his mother had described. He never talked about the war. She wouldn't have even known he'd served in the Marines or his having been in Korea were it not for his mother telling her. Back then, she wasn't strong enough to confront him to ask what was going on. Augie's periods of depression would eventually lift, and things would return to 'normal', until the next time.

By comparison, Jeanne thought Leslie's situation with Will was much more complicated. Will had suffered the loss of a leg and an almost life threatening infection. No one knew what kind of devastating trauma he'd gone through at the hands of his captors. As if those things weren't enough, he was just getting over being sick as hell with malaria. Jeanne was coming to the realization Will and Tim's problems were challenges for all of them. She remembered how, a few years earlier, Will and Leslie had left their home school in Illinois. They'd come up here to run the resort during the several months Jeanne had to undergo cancer therapy. They'd risked postponing their high school graduations for a year. It was pay-back time. She and Augie had needed them then. Will and Leslie and Tim needed them now. She was sure Augie would agree. *He's probably already come to the same conclusion.*

Coming Soon!

"Phantom Tracks"
Book Five In the Series